# 新編
# 成人英語課程
# ENGLISH COURSE
## for Adults

**New Edition**

舒盛宗編著

萬里機構・萬里書店出版

# 新編成人英語課程（1）

編著
赴盛宗

責任編輯
阿柿　Eva Lam

封面設計
王妙玲

版面設計
黎品先

出版者
萬里機構出版有限公司
香港鰂魚涌英皇道1065號東達中心1305室
電話：2564 7511
傳真：2565 5539
電郵：info@wanlibk.com
網址：http://www.wanlibk.com
　　　http://www.facebook.com/wanlibk

發行者
香港聯合書刊物流有限公司
香港新界大埔汀麗路36號
中華商務印刷大廈3字樓
電話：2150 2100
傳真：2407 3062
電郵：info@suplogistics.com.hk

承印者
中華商務彩色印刷有限公司

出版日期
二零一二年四月第一次印刷
二零一九年四月第二次印刷

萬里機構

萬里 Facebook

# 編輯例言

這套課本顧名思義，是專為成年人學英語而編寫的。

成年人學習外語，理解力較強，記憶力則較差；由於平日事務紛紜，學習時間不夠充裕。因此，編寫成年人的英語課本，與學校課本不同。內容要精簡，要切合成年人的生活，要基礎與應用並重。

這套課本全套共有兩冊，各冊均附 QR code 記錄讀音。課文內容大體如下：

第一冊是基礎課程。從字母發音學起，學習常用詞的讀音、句子的語調、句子的結構與句式變化等，課文精簡而有系統，易於學習。

為了克服成年人記憶力差、發音生硬的弱點，書中還編入句型練習（Sentence pattern drill），讀者可跟着 QR code 內記載的讀音，反覆練習，直至大部分句子能記在腦中，信口説出，清楚流暢。這是學習講英語（Spoken English）最有效的方法。

所有課文都以英文、中文對照形式編排，便於自學。

讀者對每一課都必須學至完全能夠聽得懂、讀得熟，才學習下一課，這樣穩紮穩打，就能收到實效。

# 目錄

## 字母 Alphaphets

🎧 0001.mp3

| 大寫 | 小寫 | 拼音 |
|------|------|------|
| A | a | /eɪ/ |
| B | b | /biː/ |
| C | c | /siː/ |
| D | d | /diː/ |
| E | e | /iː/ |
| F | f | /ef/ |
| G | g | /dʒiː/ |
| H | h | /eɪtʃ/ |
| I | i | /aɪ/ |
| J | j | /dʒeɪ/ |
| K | k | /keɪ/ |
| L | l | /el/ |
| M | m | /em/ |

| 大寫 | 小寫 | 拼音 |
|------|------|------|
| N | n | /en/ |
| O | o | /əʊ/ |
| P | p | /piː/ |
| Q | q | /kjuː/ |
| R | r | /aː(r)/ |
| S | s | /es/ |
| T | t | /tiː/ |
| U | u | /juː/ |
| V | v | /viː/ |
| W | w | /dʌbljuː/ |
| X | x | /eks/ |
| Y | y | /waɪ/ |
| Z | z | /zed/; (US)/ziː/ |

## 香港人發英文字母讀音的常見錯誤

### "單音節"讀成"雙音節"

在二十六個英文字母的發音中，只有"W"是個多音節字母，其餘都是單音節，很多港人卻把"單音節"的英文字母讀成"雙音節"，常見例子如下：

**F** /ef/

"F"常被讀成"air、芙"兩個音 /e'fu:/，字母"F"的讀音只有一個音節，是由元音 /e/ + 子音 /f/ 構成，/f/ 只是後綴氣音，不應讀成重音 /e'fu:/。

**L** /el/

"L"常被讀成"air、爐"兩個音 /e'nəʊ/，字母"F"的讀音只有一個音節，是由元音 /e/ + 子音 /l/ 構成，/l/ 只是後綴氣音，不應讀成重音 /e'nəʊ/。

**R** /a:(r)/

"R"常被讀成"丫、爐"兩個音 /a:'nəʊ/，字母"R"的讀音只有一個音節，是由元音 /a:/ + 子音 /r/ 構成，/(r)/ 音出現在括弧中表示此音在單詞中是不發音的。

**X** /eks/

"X"常被讀成"egg、匙"兩個音 /ek'si:/，字母"X"的讀音只有一個音節，是由元音 /e/ + 子音 /k/ 與 /s/ 構成，/ks/ 只是後綴氣音，不應讀成重音 /si:/。

## 錯讀字母發音

**H** /eɪtʃ/

很多港人把"H"字母讀成"egg、廚"兩個音 /eɡˈtʃjuː/，上面已說過，字母"H"的讀音也是只有一個音節，是由元音 /eɪ/ + 子音 /tʃ/ 構成，/tʃ/ 只是後綴氣音，不應讀成重音 /tʃjuː/。另外"H"的元音部份是 /eɪ/，發成字母"A"的讀音，不應發成"egg"的讀音。同樣道理，港人常把英文數目字"eight"(8) 讀成 egg-t /eɡt/ 也是錯讀，應讀"A-t"/eɪt/，請讀者多加留意。

**Q** /kjuː/

很多港人把"Q"字母讀成 kill /kɪl/（殺人），但其實"Q"的元音應發成 /juː/，即字母"U"的發音。

**W** /dʌbljuː/

上面已說過，"W"是在二十六個英文字母中唯一的多音節字母，很多港人誤讀成"耷 -B-U"。但是"W"應讀作"double U"/dʌbljuː/，只因"w"是兩個"u"字的合成，因此其讀音就是"double（兩個、雙重）的 u"。

**Z** /zed/; (US)/ziː/

不知何解，很多港人把"Z"字母讀成"二、said"，其實應發成"zaid"/zed/ 或美式的"zee"/ziː/。

＊關於英語國際音標，請參考本書附錄。

## 數字 Numbers

0002.mp3

| | | |
|---|---|---|
| one | 一 | 1 |
| two | 二 | 2 |
| three | 三 | 3 |
| four | 四 | 4 |
| five | 五 | 5 |
| six | 六 | 6 |
| seven | 七 | 7 |
| eight | 八 | 8 |
| nine | 九 | 9 |
| ten | 十 | 10 |
| eleven | 十一 | 11 |
| twelve | 十二 | 12 |
| thirteen | 十三 | 13 |
| fourteen | 十四 | 14 |
| fifteen | 十五 | 15 |
| twenty | 二十 | 20 |
| twenty-one | 二十一 | 21 |
| thirty | 三十 | 30 |
| forty | 四十 | 40 |
| fifty | 五十 | 50 |
| sixty | 六十 | 60 |
| seventy | 七十 | 70 |

| eighty | 八十 | 80 |
|---|---|---|
| ninty | 九十 | 90 |
| one hundred | 一百 | 100 |
| one hundred and eighty-seven | 一百八十七 | 187 |
| one thousand | 一千 | 1,000 |
| ten thousand | 一萬 | 10,000 |
| one hundred thousand | 十萬 | 100,000 |
| one million | 一百萬 | 1,000,000 |
| ten million | 一千萬 | 10,000,000 |
| one hundred million | 一億 | 100,000,000 |
| one billion | 十億 | 1,000,000,000 |
| zero | 零 | 0 |

## 身體 The Human Body

🎧 0003.mp3

| armpit | 腋窩 |
|---|---|
| head | 頭 |
| hair | 頭髮 |
| face | 臉 |
| elbow | 手肘 |
| eye | 眼睛 |
| ear | 耳朵 |

| | |
|---|---|
| knee | 膝蓋 |
| mouth | 嘴巴 |
| navel / belly button | 肚臍 |
| tooth, teeth | 牙齒 |
| nose | 鼻子 |
| neck | 脖子 |
| shoulder | 肩膀 |
| waist | 腰 |
| wrist | 手腕 |
| arm | 手臂 |
| hand | 手 |
| finger | 手指 |
| leg | 腿 |
| foot, feet | 腳 |
| toe | 腳趾 |

## 星期、月份、季節、節慶

### 星期與月份 Days and Months

🎧 0004.mp3

| 全寫 | 縮寫 | 中譯 |
|---|---|---|
| Monday | MON | 星期一 |
| Tuesday | TUE | 星期二 |
| Wednesday | WED | 星期三 |

| | | |
|---|---|---|
| Thursday | THU | 星期四 |
| Friday | FRI | 星期五 |
| Saturday | SAT | 星期六 |
| Sunday | SUN | 星期日 |
| January | JAN | 一月 |
| February | FEB | 二月 |
| March | MAR | 三月 |
| April | APR | 四月 |
| May | MAY | 五月 |
| June | JUN | 六月 |
| July | JUL | 七月 |
| August | AUG | 八月 |
| September | SEP | 九月 |
| October | OCT | 十月 |
| November | NOV | 十一月 |
| December | DEC | 十二月 |

## 季節與節慶 Seasons and Festival

🎧 0005.mp3

| | |
|---|---|
| spring | 春天 |
| summer | 夏天 |
| autumn（英）/fall（美） | 秋天 |
| winter | 冬天 |

| | |
|---|---|
| New Year | 新曆元旦 |
| Lunar New Year | 農曆新年 |
| Ching Ming Festival | 清明節 |
| Easter | 復活節 |
| Dragon-Boat Festival | 龍舟節（端午節） |
| Mid Autumn Festival | 中秋節 |
| National Day | 國慶日 |
| Winter solstice | 冬至 |
| Christmas Eve | 平安夜（聖誕前夕） |
| Christmas Day | 聖誕節 |

## 家庭 Family

🎧 0006.mp3

| | |
|---|---|
| grandparents | 祖父母 |
| grandfather | 祖父 |
| grandmother | 祖母 |
| parents | 父母 |
| father | 父親 |
| mother | 母親 |
| son | 兒子 |
| daughter | 女兒 |
| man, men | 男人 |
| uncle | 叔、伯、姨丈、舅父 |
| woman, women | 女人 |

| aunt | 嬸母、伯母、姨母、舅母 |
| brother | 兄弟 |
| boy | 男孩子 |
| sister | 姊妹 |
| girl | 女孩子 |
| cousin | 表兄弟、表姊妹 |
| husband | 丈夫 |
| wife, wives | 妻子 |
| baby, babies | 嬰兒 |
| child, children | 小孩子 |
| father / mother（in law） | 公婆、岳父母 |
| son / daughter（in law） | 女婿、媳婦 |

✽名詞由單數轉為複數時，通常在詞尾後加 -s; 有些例外的，本節則將其複數形式列出，以供讀者參考。

## 餐點、餐廳、餐具

### 餐點 Meals

🎧 0007.mp3

| breakfast | 早餐 |
| lunch | 午飯 |
| brunch | 早午餐（早午兩餐拼合一餐吃） |
| dinner | 中午或晚上吃的主餐 |
| supper | 晚餐 |

## 餐廳 Restaurant

🎧 0008.mp3

| café | 咖啡室 |
| --- | --- |
| fast food shop | 快餐店 |
| Big Fairwood | 大快活 |
| Café de Coral | 大家樂 |
| Maxim Restaurant | 美心餐廳 |

## 餐具 Tableware

🎧 0009.mp3

| chopsticks | 筷子 |
| --- | --- |
| cup | 茶杯 |
| glass | 玻璃杯 |
| plate/dish | 碟 / 盤子 |
| spoon | 匙 |
| knife, knives | 刀 |
| fork | 叉 |

## 食物與調味品
## 肉食 Meat

🎧 0010.mp3

| bacon | 烟肉 |
| --- | --- |
| chicken | 雞 |

| | |
|---|---|
| meatball | 肉丸 |
| lamb chop | 羊扒 |
| pork chop | 豬扒 |
| ribs | 排骨 |
| steak | 牛扒 |
| ox tongue | 牛脷 |
| sausage | 香腸 |

## 麵包 Bread

🎧 0011.mp3

| | |
|---|---|
| bagel | 百吉圈 |
| baguette / french stick | 法式長包 |
| croissant | 牛角包 |
| french toast | 西多士（法蘭西吐司） |
| hamburger | 漢堡包 |
| hotdog | 熱狗（香腸麵包） |
| roll | 小圓麵包 |
| butter | 牛油 |
| cheese | 芝士（乾乳酪） |
| congee / porridge / gruel | 粥 |

## 雞蛋 Egg

🎧 0012.mp3

| | |
|---|---|
| boiled egg | 烚蛋 |
| sunny side up | 太陽蛋 |
| scramble egg | 炒蛋 |
| omelette | 奄列（煎蛋捲） |

## 班戟（薄餅）Pancake

🎧 0013.mp3

| | |
|---|---|
| crêpe | 法式薄餅 |
| pizza | 意式薄餅 |

## 意大利麵條 Pasta

🎧 0014.mp3

| | |
|---|---|
| angel hair | 天使幼麵 |
| lasagna | 寬條麵 |
| macaroni | 通心粉 |
| ravioli | 意大利餛飩 |
| spaghetti | 意大利粉 |

## 中式麵條 Noodle

🎧 0015.mp3

| | |
|---|---|
| with fish ball | 魚蛋麵 |
| with shrimp dumpling | 餛飩麵 |
| with brisket | 牛腩麵 |
| with offal | 牛雜麵 |
| ramen | 日式拉麵 |

## 沙律 Salad

🎧 0016.mp3

| | |
|---|---|
| salad | 沙律（沙拉） |
| chef salad | 廚師沙律 |
| green salad | 雜菜沙律 |
| sandwich | 三文治 |
| club sandwich | 公司三文治 |

## 海鮮 Sea Food

🎧 0017.mp3

| | |
|---|---|
| fish | 魚 |
| clam | 蜆（蛤蜊） |
| crab | 蟹 |
| lobster | 龍蝦 |
| oyster | 蠔（牡蠣） |

| mussel | 青口（淡菜） |
|---|---|
| prawn（英）/ shrimp（美） | 蝦 |
| squid | 魷魚 |
| cuttlefish | 墨魚 |

## 調味料 Seasoning

🎧 0018.mp3

| butter | 牛油（黃油） |
|---|---|
| ketchup | 調味番茄醬 |
| maggie sauce | 美極鮮醬油 |
| olive oil | 橄欖油 |
| pepper | 胡椒粉 |
| salt | 鹽 |
| soya sauce | 醬油 |
| sugar | 糖 |
| vinegar | 醋 |

## 零食與甜點

### 零食 Snacks

🎧 0019.mp3

| french fries | 炸薯條 |
|---|---|
| fish-ball | 魚蛋 |

| smelly tofu | 臭豆腐 |
| fried chicken wing | 炸雞翼 |

## 西式甜點 Desserts (Western Style)

🎧 0020.mp3

| apple pie/crumble | 蘋果批（蘋果餡餅） |
| cheese cake | 芝士蛋糕 |
| crème brûlée | 焦糖燉蛋（焦糖奶油） |
| cream puffs | 忌廉泡夫（奶油夾心酥球） |
| doughnut | 冬甩（炸糖環） |
| custard tart | 蛋撻（蛋奶撻） |
| muffin | 鬆餅 |
| pancake | 班戟（薄煎餅） |
| tiramisu | 意大利蛋糕 |
| swiss roll | 瑞士卷（捲筒蛋糕） |
| waffle | 威化焗餅（華夫夾餅） |
| mango pudding | 芒果布甸（芒果布丁） |
| bread pudding | 麵包布甸（麵包布丁） |

## 中式甜點 Dessert (Chinese Style)

🎧 0021.mp3

| red bean soup | 紅豆沙 |
| sesame paste | 芝麻糊 |

| freshly ground walnut paste | 生磨合桃露 |
| peanut paste | 花生糊 |
| glutinous rice ball | 湯圓 |
| chilled mango juice with pomelo | 楊枝金露 |

## 湯與飲料

### 湯 Soup

🎧 0022.mp3

| borsch | 羅宋湯 |
| clam chowder | 周打蜆湯 |
| chicken stock | 雞湯 |
| minestrone | 意大利菜湯 |
| french onion soup | 法國洋葱湯 |
| cream of mushroom | 奶油（忌廉）磨菇湯 |
| lobster bisque | 龍蝦湯 |
| thick pea soup | 青豆湯 |

### 飲料 Beverages

🎧 0023.mp3

| coffee | 咖啡 |
| café au lait | 牛奶咖啡 |

| | |
|---|---|
| cappuccino | 肉桂粉加熱牛奶的咖啡 |
| espresso | 特濃咖啡 |
| latte | 意大利牛奶咖啡 |
| mocha | 朱古力咖啡（巧克力咖啡） |
| chocolate | 朱古力奶（巧克力奶） |
| chrysanthemum tea | 菊花茶 |
| fruit punch | 雜果賓治 |
| milk | 牛奶 |
| tea | 茶 |
| soft drink | 汽水 |

## 酒精飲料 Alcohols

🎧 0024.mp3

| | |
|---|---|
| beer | 啤酒 |
| brandy | 白蘭地 |
| wine (red / white) | 紅 / 白酒 |
| whiskey | 威士忌 |
| vodka | 伏特加 |
| cocktails | 雞尾酒 |

# 蔬果

## 水果 Fruit

🎧 0025.mp3

| | |
|---|---|
| apple | 蘋果 |
| avocado | 牛油果（鱷梨） |
| blackberry | 黑莓 |
| blueberry | 藍莓 |
| coconut | 椰子 |
| cranberry | 紅莓 |
| cherry | 車厘子（櫻桃） |
| dragon fruit（pitaya） | 火龍果 |
| durian | 榴槤 |
| honeydew melon | 哈密瓜 |
| lemon | 檸檬 |
| lime | 青檸 |
| banana | 香蕉 |
| fig | 無花果 |
| grapes | 提子（葡萄） |
| grapefruit | 西柚 |
| guava | 番石榴 |
| kiwi fruit | 奇異果（獼猴桃） |
| lychee | 荔枝 |
| mandarin | 柑 |

| | |
|---|---|
| mango | 杧果 |
| mangosteen | 山竹果 |
| olive | 橄欖 |
| orange | 橙 |
| passion fruit | 熱情果（雞蛋果） |
| raspberry | 山莓（懸鈎子） |
| papaya | 木瓜 |
| peach | 蜜桃 |
| pear | 梨 |
| pineapple | 菠蘿（鳳梨） |
| plum | 布冧、洋李（梅） |
| pomegranate | 石榴 |
| pomelo | 沙田柚（柚子） |
| starfruit | 楊桃 |
| strawberry | 士多啤梨（草莓） |
| sweet melon | 蜜瓜 |
| tangerine | 桔 |
| watermelon | 西瓜 |

## 蔬菜 Vegetable

🎧 0026.mp3

| | |
|---|---|
| asparagus | 蘆筍 |
| bean | 豆 |

23

| | |
|---|---|
| bean sprouts | 豆芽 |
| beetroot | 紅菜頭（甜菜根） |
| bitter gourd | 苦瓜（涼瓜） |
| broccoli | 西蘭花 |
| cabbage | 椰菜、黃芽白（捲心菜） |
| carrot | 甘筍（紅蘿蔔、胡蘿蔔） |
| cauliflower | 椰菜花 |
| celery | 西芹 |
| Chinese spinach | 莧菜 |
| corn on the cob | 粟米（玉米） |
| coriander | 芫荽 |
| cucumber | 青瓜（黃瓜） |
| eggplant（aubergine） | 矮瓜（茄子） |
| garlic | 蒜頭 |
| ginger | 薑 |
| leek | 韭葱 |
| lettuce | 生菜 |
| mushroom | 香菇 |
| potato | 薯仔（馬鈴薯） |
| tofu / bean curd | 豆腐 |
| tomato | 番茄 |
| onion | 洋葱 |
| peas | 豌豆 |

| | |
|---|---|
| peppers（green/ red） | 燈籠椒（紅/青） |
| pumpkin | 南瓜（番瓜） |
| spinach | 菠菜 |
| spring / green onion | 大葱 |
| sweet potato | 蕃薯（甘薯） |
| turnip /radish | 蘿蔔 |
| straw mushroom | 草菇 |
| watercress | 西洋菜 |
| water chestnut | 馬蹄（荸薺） |
| water spinach | 通菜（蕹菜） |
| wax/white gourd | 冬瓜 |

## 衣物 Clothes

🎧 0027.mp3

| | |
|---|---|
| belt | 腰帶 |
| blouse | 女裝恤衫（女裝襯衣） |
| boots | 靴 |
| bow tie | 煲呔（蝶形領結） |
| braces（英）/ suspenders（美） | 吊褲帶 |
| buckle | 腰帶扣 |
| cardigan | 開襟毛衣 |
| collar | 衣領 |
| coat | 外套 |

25

| | |
|---|---|
| cuff | 袖口 |
| dress, dresses | 衣服 |
| gloves | 手套 |
| hat | 帽子 |
| handkerchief | 手帕 |
| high heels | 高跟鞋 |
| jacket | 短外套（夾克） |
| jeans | 牛仔褲 |
| jumper | 針織套衫 |
| leggings / tights | 襪褲 |
| mitten / mittens | 連指手套 |
| nightdress（英）/ nightgown（美） | 睡袍 |
| overcoat | 長大衣 |
| pyjamas（英）/ pajamas（美） | 睡衣 |
| raincoat | 雨衣 |
| scarf | 圍巾 |
| shoes | 鞋子 |
| shirt | 男襯衣 |
| skirt | 裙子 |
| sleeve | 衫袖 |
| sweatshirt | 長袖運動衣 |
| stockings | 長襪子 |
| socks | 短襪子 |

| | |
|---|---|
| suit | 一套衣服 |
| tie（英）/ necktie（美） | 領呔（領帶） |
| tracksuit | 運動服 |
| trench coat | 乾濕褸（軍服式雨衣） |
| trousers（英）/ pants（美） | 褲子 |
| trainers（英）/ sneakers（美） | 運動鞋 |
| waistcoat(英) / vest(美) | 西服背心 |

## 顏色 Colour

🎧 0028.mp3

| | |
|---|---|
| black | 黑色 |
| blue | 藍色 |
| azure | 天藍色 |
| navy blue | 海軍藍 |
| brown | 咖啡色（褐色、棕色） |
| chocolate | 朱古力色 |
| green | 綠色 |
| gold | 金色 |
| grey | 灰色 |
| orange | 橙色 |
| pink | 粉紅色 |
| purple | 紫色 |
| violet | 藍紫色 |
| lavender | 淡紫色 |

| | |
|---|---|
| red | 紅色 |
| crimson | 深紅色 |
| scarlet | 鮮紅色 |
| silver | 銀色 |
| white | 白色 |
| beige | 米白色、米黃色 |
| cream | 奶白色 |
| ivory | 象牙白色 |
| yellow | 黃色 |
| multi-coloured | 彩色 |

## 房子與建築物

### 房子 Houses

🎧 0029.mp3

| | |
|---|---|
| kitchen | 廚房 |
| furniture | 傢具 |
| table | 桌子 |
| chair | 椅子 |
| sofa | 沙發 |
| bed | 床 |
| radio | 收音機 |
| television | 電視機 |
| refrigerator | 電冰箱 |
| telephone | 電話 |

| | |
|---|---|
| clock | 鐘 |
| door | 門 |
| wall | 牆壁 |
| floor | 地板 |
| ceiling | 天花板 |
| roof, roofs | 屋頂 |
| window | 窗子 |
| curtains | 窗簾 |
| living room | 客廳 |
| dining room | 飯廳 |
| bedroom | 睡房 |
| bathroom | 浴室 |

## 建築物 Buildings

🎧 0030.mp3

| | |
|---|---|
| school | 學校 |
| library, libraries | 圖書館 |
| park | 公園 |
| museum | 博物館 |
| theatre | 戲院 |
| hotel | 酒店，旅館 |
| department store | 百貨商店 |
| bank | 銀行 |
| post office | 郵政局 |

| police station | 警察局 |
|---|---|
| hospital | 醫院 |
| Hong Kong Disneyland | 香港迪士尼樂園 |
| railway station | 火車站 |
| airport | 飛機場 |

## 交通 Transportation

🎧 0031.mp3

| train | 火車 |
|---|---|
| underground | 地底火車，地鐵 |
| motorcycle | 電單車，摩托車 |
| highway | 公路 |
| flyover | 天橋 |
| tunnel | 隧道 |
| car | 汽車 |
| bus | 公共汽車，巴士 |
| taxi | 計程車，的士 |
| bicycle | 自行車，單車 |
| ship | 輪船 |

| ferry | 渡海小輪 |
| --- | --- |
| airplane | 飛機 |
| LRT（Light Rail Transit） | 輕便鐵路 |
| MTR（Mass Transit Railway） | 香港鐵路、地下鐵路 |
| Peak tram | 山頂纜車 |
| tram | 電車 |

## 職業 Occupations

🎧 0032.mp3

| clerk | 文員 |
| --- | --- |
| civil servant | 公務員 |
| worker | 工人 |
| farmer | 農民 |
| merchant | 商人 |
| teacher | 教師 |
| professor | 教授 |
| journalist | 新聞工作者 |
| nurse | 護士 |
| doctor | 醫生 |
| engineer | 工程師 |

## 方向 Directions

⌒ 0033.mp3

| | | |
|---|---|---|
| north | N | 北 |
| east | E | 東 |
| south | S | 南 |
| west | W | 西 |
| northeast | NE | 東北 |
| southeast | SE | 東南 |
| southwest | SW | 西南 |
| northwest | NW | 西北 |

# CHAPTER 01

## This is a pen

這是一枝鋼筆

**本課目標**

學會以英語陳述及提問

# 文法及用法分析

## 陳述句："這是×××。"

🎧 0101.mp3

| | |
|---|---|
| This is a pen ↘ . | 這是一枝鋼筆。 |
| That is an apple ↘ . | 那是一個蘋果。 |
| It is a dog ↘ . | 這是一隻狗。 |

"This is ..."是英語中最簡單的陳述句句型。This為主語，is為動詞。轉為疑問句的時候，要將動詞和主語的次序倒轉，成為"Is this ...？"。This指較為近一點的事物，而that則指遠一點的事物。

## 疑問句："這是 ××× 嗎？"

🎧 0102.mp3

| | |
|---|---|
| Is this a book ↗ ? | 這是一本書嗎？ |
| Yes ↘ , it is ↘ . | 是的，這是。 |
| Is that a desk ↗ ? | 那是一張書桌嗎？ |
| No ↘ , it is not ↘ . | 不，這不是。 |
| Is it a chair ↗ ? | 這是一張椅子嗎？ |
| No ↘ , it isn't ↘ . | 不，這不是。 |

要回答上面所提到的疑問句時，可以用簡略的回答：

Yes, it is. ，No, it is not(isn't). ，即是將被問到的名詞省略掉。Yes為肯定，No為否定，isn't為is not的縮寫。

## 問句結尾要變調

🎧 0103.mp3

| | |
|---|---|
| What is this ↘ ? | 這是甚麼？ |
| It is a flower ↘ . | 這是一朵花。 |
| What colour is it ↘ ? | 它是甚麼顏色的？ |
| It is red ↘ . | 它是紅色的。 |
| The flower is red ↘ . | 這朵花是紅色的。 |

疑問句結尾一般都用升調，例如Is this a book↗？但帶有疑問詞（如
What，When，Where，Why，Who，Whose等等）的疑問句一般
都用降調，例如What is this ↘ ？。

## 冠詞：中文沒有的名詞修飾

注意冠詞a，an和the的用法。a，an為不定冠詞，用於指一般的
人或事物，名詞的開首為子音時用a，例如a pen（一枝鋼筆），a
flower（一朵花）；為母音時用an，例如an apple（一個蘋果），an egg
（一隻雞蛋）；如果名詞前面的形容詞亦以母音開首，要用an，例
如an old man（一個老年人），an honest boy（一個誠實的男孩子）。
the為指定冠詞，用於指特定的人或事物。

# 句型練習

請把左右兩欄片語拼成完整句子。

🎧 0104.mp3

| This is | | a pen |
|---------|---|-------|
| That's | | a book |
| Is this | + | a desk |
| It's | | a chair |
| Is that | | a notebook |

**This is**
1. This is a pen.
2. This is a book.
3. This is a desk.
4. This is a chair.
5. This is a notebook.

**That's**
6. That's a pen.
7. That's a book.
8. That's a desk.
9. That's a chair.
10. That's a notebook.

**Is this**
11. Is this a pen?
12. Is this a book?
13. Is this a desk?
14. Is this a chair?
15. Is this a notebook?

**It's**
16. It's a pen.
17. It's a book.
18. It's a desk.
19. It's a chair.
20. It's a notebook.

**Is that**
21. Is that a pen?
22. Is that a book?
23. Is that a desk?
24. Is that a chair?
25. Is that a notebook?

請把左右兩欄片語拼成完整句子。

🎧 0105.mp3

Ch 01

| This isn't | | a chair |
|---|---|---|
| Isn't this | | a door |
| That isn't | + | a wall |
| Isn't that | | a table |
| It isn't | | a window |

### This isn't

1. This isn't a chair.
2. This isn't a door.
3. This isn't a wall.
4. This isn't a table.
5. This isn't a window.

### Isn't this

6. Isn't this a chair?
7. Isn't this a door?
8. Isn't this a wall?
9. Isn't this a table?
10. Isn't this a window?

### That isn't

11. That isn't a chair.
12. That isn't a door.
13. That isn't a wall.
14. That isn't a table.
15. That isn't a window.

### Isn't that

16. Isn't that a chair?
17. Isn't that a door?
18. Isn't that a wall?
19. Isn't that a table?
20. Isn't that a window?

### It isn't

21. It isn't a chair.
22. It isn't a door.
23. It isn't a wall.
24. It isn't a table.
25. It isn't a window.

# 句型變化

🎧 0106.mp3

| This is a small knife. | 這是一把小的刀。 |
| This knife is small. | 這把刀是小的。 |
| This is a large window. | 這是一扇大的窗戶。 |
| This window is large. | 這窗戶是大的。 |
| This is a red flower. | 這是一朵紅色的花。 |
| This flower is red. | 這朵花是紅色的。 |
| That's a large knife. | 那是一把大的刀。 |
| That knife is large. | 那把刀是大的。 |
| That's a small window. | 那是一扇小的窗戶。 |
| That window is small. | 那扇窗戶是小的。 |
| That's a purple pencil. | 那是一枝紫色的鉛筆。 |
| That pencil is purple. | 那枝鉛筆是紫色的。 |
| That's a piece of red paper. | 那是一張紅色的紙。 |
| That piece of paper is red. | 那張紙是紅色的。 |
| That's a piece of white chalk. | 那是一根白色的粉筆。 |
| That piece of chalk is white. | 那根粉筆是白色的。 |
| Is this a small desk? | 這是一張小的書桌嗎？ |
| Is this desk small? | 這書桌是小的嗎？ |
| Is this a blue skirt? | 這是一條藍色的裙子嗎？ |
| Is this skirt blue? | 這條裙子是藍色的嗎？ |

# CHAPTER 02

## I am a girl

我是一個女孩子

**本課目標**

學會運用代名詞介紹自己和別人

# 文法及用法分析

## 代名詞：英文中的 "你我他"

⌒ 0201.mp3

| | |
|---|---|
| I am a girl ↘ . | 我是（一個）女孩子。 |
| You are a boy ↘ . | 你是（一個）男孩子。 |
| She is a teacher ↘ . | 她是（一位）老師。 |
| He is a student ↘ . | 他是（一個）學生。 |
| They are schoolboys ↘ . | 他們是男學生。 |
| We are schoolgirls ↘ . | 我們是女學生。 |

I，you，he，she，we，they 等都是人稱代名詞（personal pronouns），在句子作主詞。

I 代表講話的人，為第一人稱（first person）；

you 代表對講的人，為第二人稱（second person）；

he，she 代表所講及的人，為第三人稱（third person）。

we 為第一人稱複數，you 為第二人稱複數，they 為第三人稱複數。

## 動詞 be

⌒ 0202.mp3

| | |
|---|---|
| What's your name ↘ ? | 你的名字叫甚麼？ |
| My name is Tom ↘ . | 我的名字叫湯姆。 |

動詞 be 要跟隨人稱和數的變化而變化：I 用 am；you，we，they 用 are；he，she 用 is。另外 it 字是代表死物的代名詞，屬第三人稱，所以用 is。

## 代名詞 +not / be 的縮寫

🎧 0203.mp3

| | |
|---|---|
| Are you a doctor ↗ ? | 你是（一位）醫生嗎？ |
| Yes ↘ , I am ↘ . | 是，我是 |
| No ↘ , I'm not ↘ . | 不，我不是。 |
| Is she a nurse ↗ ? | 她是一位護士嗎？ |
| Yes ↘ , she is ↘ . | 是的，她是。 |
| No ↘ , she isn't ↘ . | 不，她不是。 |
| What's her job ↘ ? | 她是幹甚麼的？ |
| She is a clerk ↘ . | 她是一位文員。 |

代名詞和 not 字與 be 連用時，有時應用縮寫的形式，這些形式在會話裏十分普遍。以下為最常見的縮寫：

| | |
|---|---|
| I am = I'm | you are = you're |
| he is = he's | she is = she's |
| it is = it's | we are = we're |
| they are = they're | is not = isn't |
| are not = aren't | |

# 句型練習

請把左右兩欄片語拼成完整句子。

🎧 0204.mp3

| I'm | | a teacher |
|---|---|---|
| Am I | | a student |
| I'm not | + | a schoolboy |
| Are you | | a schoolgirl |
| You're | | a high school student |

## I'm

❶ I'm a teacher.
❷ I'm a student.
❸ I'm a schoolboy.
❹ I'm a schoolgirl.
❺ I'm a high school student.

## Am I

❻ Am I a teacher?
❼ Am I a student?
❽ Am I a schoolboy?
❾ Am I a schoolgirl?
❿ Am I a high school student?

## I'm not

⓫ I'm not a teacher.
⓬ I'm not a student.
⓭ I'm not a schoolboy.
⓮ I'm not a schoolgirl.
⓯ I'm not a high school student.

## Are you

⓰ Are you a teacher?
⓱ Are you a student?
⓲ Are you a schoolboy?
⓳ Are you a schoolgirl?
⓴ Are you a high school student?

## You're

㉑ You're a teacher.
㉒ You're a student.
㉓ You're a schoolboy.
㉔ You're a schoolgirl.
㉕ You're a high school student.

請把左右兩欄片語拼成完整句子。

🎧 0205.mp3

| My name is | |
| My name isn't | John Brown |
| Your name is | Jim Green |
| Is your name | + Tom Black |
| His name is | Bob White |
| | Fred Gray |

**My name is**

❶ My name is John Brown.
❷ My name is Jim Green.
❸ My name is Tom Black.
❹ My name is Bob White.
❺ My name is Fred Gray.

**My name isn't**

❻ My name isn't John Brown.
❼ My name isn't Jim Green.
❽ My name isn't Tom Black.
❾ My name isn't Bob White.
❿ My name isn't Fred Gray.

**Your name is**

⑪ Your name is John Brown.
⑫ Your name is Jim Green.
⑬ Your name is Tom Black.
⑭ Your name is Bob White.
⑮ Your name is Fred Gray.

**Is your name**

⑯ Is your name John Brown?
⑰ Is your name Jim Green?
⑱ Is your name Tom Black?
⑲ Is your name Bob White?
⑳ Is your name Fred Gray?

**His name is**

㉑ His name is John Brown.
㉒ His name is Jim Green.
㉓ His name is Tom Black.
㉔ His name is Bob White.
㉕ His name is Fred Gray.

# 句型變化

🎧 0206.mp3

| | |
|---|---|
| I'm Jack Andrews. | 我是傑克‧安德魯。 |
| My name is Jack Andrews. | 我的名字是傑克‧安德魯。 |
| I'm Paul Smith. | 我是保羅‧史密斯。 |
| My name is Paul Smith. | 我的名字是保羅‧史密斯。 |
| Are you Jack Andrews? | 你是傑克‧安德魯嗎？ |
| Is your name Jack Andrews? | 你的名字是傑克‧安德魯嗎？ |
| Are you Paul Smith? | 你是保羅‧史密斯嗎？ |
| Is your name Paul Smith? | 你的名字是保羅‧史密斯嗎？ |
| He is Tom Brown. | 他是湯姆‧布朗。 |
| His name is Tom Brown. | 他的名字是湯姆‧布朗。 |
| He is Jim Green. | 他是占姆‧格林。 |
| His name is Jim Green. | 他的名字是占姆‧格林。 |
| She is Judy. | 她是朱迪。 |
| Her name is Judy. | 她的名字是朱迪。 |
| She is Mary White. | 她是瑪麗‧懷特。 |
| Her name is Mary White. | 她的名字是瑪麗‧懷特。 |
| She isn't Judy. | 她不是朱迪。 |
| Her name isn't Judy. | 她的名字不是朱迪。 |
| She isn't Mary White. | 她不是瑪麗‧懷特。 |
| Her name isn't Mary White. | 她的名字不是瑪麗‧懷特。 |

# CHAPTER 03

## This is my pen

### 這是我的鋼筆

**本課目標**

學會運用 "所有形容詞" 和
"所有代名詞" 說明 "所有權"

# 文法及用法分析

## 所有形容詞：表示事物持有人

🎧 0301.mp3

| | |
|---|---|
| This is my pen ↘ . | 這是我的鋼筆。 |
| It's mine ↘ . | 這是我的。 |
| That's your pencil ↘ . | 那是你的鉛筆。 |
| It's yours ↘ . | 那是你的。 |
| She is my mother. | 她是我的母親。 |
| They are our teachers. | 他們是我們的老師。 |

my，your，his，her，its，our，their 等都是所有形容詞（possessive adjectives），是能夠表示出一件事物的持有人的形容詞。例句中，my，your，our 分別形容 pen，pencil，mother，teachers 等名詞，指出這些人或物之所屬。

## 名詞 +'s 表示事物持有人

🎧 0302.mp3

| | |
|---|---|
| This is my sister's book. | 這是我妹妹的書。 |
| The girl's pencil is blue. | 這個女孩子的鉛筆是藍色的。 |

這裏順便介紹另一種表達事物持有人的句型：

從以上的例句可以見到，只要在名詞末尾加上 "'s"，便可以表示出物件的所有者。

## 所有代名詞：代表某某持有的東西

🎧 0303.mp3

| | |
|---|---|
| Is this book yours ↘ ? | 這本書是你的嗎？ |
| Yes ↘ , it's mine ↘ . | 是的，這是我的。 |
| No ↘ , it isn't mine ↘ . | 不是，這不是我的。 |
| Whose dog is it ↘ ? | 這只狗是誰的？ |
| It's his dog ↘ . | 這是他的狗。 |
| It's his ↘ . | 這是他的。 |
| Whose car is it ↘ ? | 這輛車是誰的？ |
| It's her car ↘ . | 這是她的車。 |
| It's hers ↘ . | 這是她的。 |
| It's our car ↘ . | 這是我們的車。 |
| It's ours ↘ . | 這是我們的。 |
| It is their car ↘ . | 這是他們的車。 |
| It's theirs ↘ . | 這是他們的。 |

mine、yours、his、hers、its、ours、theirs 等都是所有代名詞（possessive pronouns）。例如：

| | |
|---|---|
| That is Mary's desk. | 那是瑪麗的書桌。 |
| It is hers. | 這是她的。 |
| This is my room. | 這是我的房間。 |
| It is mine. | 這是我的。 |

在以上的例句裏，hers 及 mine 作為代名詞，分別代替了 Mary's desk 及 my room。下面是所有形容詞及其相對的所有代名司：

| | | | |
|---|---|---|---|
| my —— mine | | your —— yours |
| his —— his | | her —— hers |
| its —— its | | our —— ours |
| their —— theirs | | |

# 句型練習

請把左右兩欄片語拼成完整句子。

🎧 0304.mp3

| | | |
|---|---|---|
| This is | | Mr. Brown |
| Are you | | Mrs. White |
| I'm | + | Miss Gray |
| Aren't you | | Mrs. Black |
| I'm not | | Miss Green |

## This is

1 This is Mr. Brown.
2 This is Mrs. White.
3 This is Miss Gray.
4 This is Mrs. Black.
5 This is Miss Green.

## Are you

6 Are you Mr. Brown?
7 Are you Mrs. White?
8 Are you Miss Gray?
9 Are you Mrs. Black?
10 Are you Miss Green?

## I'm

11 I'm Mr. Brown.
12 I'm Mrs. White.
13 I'm Miss Gray.
14 I'm Mrs. Black.
15 I'm Miss Green.

## Aren't you

16 Aren't you Mr. Brown?
17 Aren't you Mrs. White?
18 Aren't you Miss Gray?
19 Aren't you Mrs. Black?
20 Aren't you Miss Green?

## I'm not

21 I'm not Mr. Brown.
22 I'm not Mrs. White.
23 I'm not Miss Gray.
24 I'm not Mrs. Black.
25 I'm not Miss Green.

請把左右兩欄片語拼成完整句子。

🎧 0305.mp3

| | | |
|---|---|---|
| This is | | mine |
| Isn't that | | yours |
| That's | + | his |
| Is it | | hers |
| It isn't | | my sister's |

**This is**
1. This is mine.
2. This is yours.
3. This is his.
4. This is hers.
5. This is my sister's.

**Isn't that**
6. Isn't that mine?
7. Isn't that yours?
8. Isn't that his?
9. Isn't that hers?
10. Isn't that my sister's?

**That's**
11. That's mine.
12. That's yours.
13. That's his.
14. That's hers.
15. That's my sister's.

**Is it**
16. Is it mine?
17. Is it yours?
18. Is it his?
19. Is it hers?
20. Is it my sister's?

**It isn't**
21. It isn't mine.
22. It isn't yours.
23. It isn't his.
24. It isn't hers.
25. It isn't my sister's.

🎧 0306.mp3

| | |
|---|---|
| This is my pencil. | 這是我的鉛筆。 |
| This pencil is mine. | 這枝鉛筆是我的。 |
| This is your knife. | 這是你的刀。 |
| This knife is yours. | 這把刀是你的。 |
| This is his package. | 這是他的包裹。 |
| This package is his. | 這包裹是他的。 |
| This is her desk. | 這是她的書桌。 |
| This desk is hers. | 這張書桌是她的。 |
| This is my sister's coat. | 這是我妹妹（姊姊）的外套。 |
| This coat is my sister's. | 這件外套是我妹妹（姊姊）的。 |
| This is Mr. Brown's notebook. | 這是布朗先生的筆記簿。 |
| This notebook is Mr. Brown's. | 這本筆記簿是布朗先生的。 |
| This is our room. | 這我們的房間。 |
| This room is ours. | 這房間是我們的。 |
| This is my pencil. | 這是我的鉛筆。 |
| This pencil is mine. | 這枝鉛筆是我的。 |
| This is your knife. | 這是你的刀。 |
| This knife is yours. | 這把刀是你的。 |
| This is his package. | 這是他的包裹。 |
| This package is his. | 這包裹是他的。 |
| This is her desk. | 這是她的書桌。 |
| This desk is hers. | 這張書桌是她的。 |
| This is my sister's coat. | 這是我妹妹（姊姊）的外套。 |
| This coat is my sister's. | 這件外套是我妹妹（姊姊）的。 |
| This is Mr. Brown's notebook. | 這是布朗先生的筆記簿。 |
| This notebook is Mr. Brown's. | 這本筆記簿是布朗先生的。 |
| This is our room. | 這我們的房間。 |
| This room is ours. | 這房間是我們的。 |

# CHAPTER 04

## There are pens

這些是鋼筆

**本課目標**

① 學會運用指示代名詞
② 學會運用基本量詞，並詢問數量

# 文法及用法分析

## 指示代名詞：this, these, that, those, there

0401.mp3

| | |
|---|---|
| This is a pen ＼. | 這是一枝鋼筆。 |
| These are pens ＼. | 這些是鋼筆。 |
| That's a book ＼. | 那是一本書。 |
| Those are books ＼. | 那些是書。 |
| There is a glass on the table ＼. | 桌子上有一隻玻璃杯。 |
| Is there a cup on the table ／? | 桌子上有一隻茶杯嗎？ |
| Yes ＼, there is ＼. | 有的，那裏有。 |
| No ＼, there isn't ＼. | 沒有，那沒有。 |

here 和 there 都是表示地方和方向的副詞（adverbs）。例如：

| | |
|---|---|
| Sit there. | 坐在那。 |
| I live here. | 我住在這。 |

但是 here 和 there 很多時候都放在句首，用於引起句子，經常和動詞 be 連用：

| | |
|---|---|
| There is someone at the door. | 有人在門口。 |
| There seems to be no doubt about it. | 此事似乎無可置疑。 |
| Here's your book. | 這是你的書。 |
| Here comes the train. | 火車來了。 |
| Here it comes. | 它來了。 |

以上的例句，除了第5句外，動詞都是放在主語的前面。當主語為單數時，要用單數形式的動詞，主語為複數時，則用複數形式，例：There are many books on the desk.（桌子上有很多書。）There 字要輕讀，讀作 /ð/。

## 指示代名詞：some, any

🎧 0402.mp3

| | |
|---|---|
| Here is a book ↘. | 這裏有一本書。 |
| Here are some books ↘. | 這裏有些書。 |
| Are there any books on the table ↗? | 桌子上有沒有書呢？ |
| Yes ↘, there are some ↘. | 有的，有一些。 |
| No ↘, there aren't any ↘. | 沒有，一本也沒有。 |

一般來説，some用於肯定句中，any則用於否定句及疑問句，例如：

| | |
|---|---|
| There are some chairs in the room. | 房間裏有些椅子。 |
| There are not any chairs in the room. | 房間裏一張椅子也沒有。 |
| Are there any chairs in the room? | 房間裏有沒有椅子？ |

但是在疑問句裏，有時也可以用some：

| | |
|---|---|
| Are there some chairs in the room? | 房間裏有些椅子嗎？ |

## 詢問數量：How many / How much...?

🎧 0403.mp3

| | |
|---|---|
| How many books are there on the table ↘? | 桌子上有多少本書？ |
| There are five books ↘. | 那裏有五本書。 |

回答 "How many ... ?" 形式的句子時，要用數詞：

| How many children are there on the playground? | 操場上有多少個孩子？ |
|---|---|
| There are ten children. | 有十個孩子。 |
| How long is that ruler? | 這把尺有多長？ |
| It's one metre long. | 有一公尺長。 |
| How high is that mountain? | 那座山有多高？ |
| It's five hundred metres high. | 有五百公尺高。 |
| How old are you? | 你幾多歲？ |
| I'm ten years old. | 我十歲。 |

名詞分為可數及不可數兩種。"How many" 用於可數名詞，不可數名詞則用 "How much"：

| How much money do you have? | 你有多少錢？ |
|---|---|
| Oh, just a little. | 噢，只有一點點。 |

# 句型練習

請把左右兩欄片語拼成完整句子。

🎧 0404.mp3

| These are | | ours |
|---|---|---|
| These aren't | | yours |
| They are | + | theirs |
| Are they | | full |
| Aren't these | | empty |

**These are**

① These are ours.
② These are yours.
③ These are theirs.
④ These are full.
⑤ These are empty.

**Those aren't**

⑥ Those aren't ours.
⑦ Those aren't yours.
⑧ Those aren't theirs.
⑨ Those aren't full.
⑩ Those aren't empty.

**They are**

⑪ They are ours.
⑫ They are yours.
⑬ They are theirs.
⑭ They are full.
⑮ They are empty.

**Are they**

⑯ Are they ours?
⑰ Are they yours?
⑱ Are they theirs?
⑲ Are they full?
⑳ Are they empty?

**Aren't these**

㉑ Aren't these ours?
㉒ Aren't these yours?
㉓ Aren't these theirs?
㉔ Aren't these full?
㉕ Aren't these empty?

Ch04

# 句型變化

| Are there any books on the table? | 桌子上有書嗎？ |
| There are some books on the table. | 桌子上有一些書。 |
| Are there any workers in the factory? | 工廠裏有工人嗎？ |
| There are some workers in the factory. | 工廠裏有一些工人。 |
| Are there any students in the library? | 圖書館裏有學生嗎？ |
| There are some students in the library. | 圖書館裏有一些學生。 |
| Are there any children in the park? | 公園裏有小孩子嗎？ |
| There are some children in the park. | 公園裏有一些小孩子。 |
| There are some flowers in the vase. | 花瓶裏有一些花。 |
| There aren't any flowers in the vase. | 花瓶裏沒有花。 |
| There are some chairs near the window. | 窗子附近有一些椅子。 |
| There aren't any chairs near the window. | 窗子附近沒有椅子。 |
| There are some teachers in the room. | 房間裏有一些教師。 |
| There aren't any teachers in the room. | 房間裏沒有教師。 |

# CHAPTER 05

## I have a brother

我有個弟弟

**本課目標**

①學會名詞的單數與複數
②學會運用動詞have

# 文法及用法分析

## 名詞的單數、複數

∩ 0501.mp3

| | |
|---|---|
| I have a brother ﹨. | 我有一個兄弟。 |
| You have two sisters ﹨. | 你有兩個姊妹。 |
| He has a daughter ﹨. | 他有一個女兒。 |
| They have several children ﹨. | 他們有幾個孩子。 |

英語中名詞有單數和複數之分。將單數轉為複數有如下的規則：

❶ 一般的名詞由單數變成複數，只要在詞尾加上 -s，例如：

girl —— girls（女孩子）　　　　house —— houses（房子）

dog —— dogs（狗）

❷ 以 -o，-s，-ss，-sh，-ch，-x，或 -z 結尾的名詞，由單數變為複數，要在詞尾加上 -es，例如：

tomato —— tomatoes（番茄）　　bus —— buses（公共汽車）

class —— classes（班）　　　　dish —— dishes（碟子）

inch —— inches（英寸）　　　　box —— boxes（盒子）

buzz —— buzzes（嗡嗡聲）

有些以 -o 結尾的名詞只加 -s，不加 -es，例如

piano —— pianos（鋼琴）　　　　zoo —— zoos（動物園）

❸ 以 -y 結尾，而在 -y 之前的一個字母又是子音的名詞，將 -y 轉為 -i，再加 es。例如：

city —— cities（城市）　　　　lady —— ladies（淑女）

如果 -y 之前的字母是母音的話，只需加上 -s, 例如：

monkey —— monkeys（猴子）　　　　day —— days（日）

④ 以 -f 或 -fe 結尾的名詞，將 -f 或 -fe 刪掉，再加 -ves，例如：

wife —— wives（妻子）　　　　knife —— knives（刀）

half —— halves（半）

⑤ 有些名詞由單數變為複數，要改變名詞中的母音，例如：

foot —— feet（足）　　　　man —— men（男人）

woman —— women（女人）　　tooth —— teeth（牙齒）

⑥ 另外有一些不規則的轉法，例如加 -en（ox —— oxen 雄牛）；有些名詞的單複數是同一形式的，如 fish，sheep，salmon；一些從拉丁語或希臘語轉借過來的名詞仍然保持它原來的複數形式：

datum —— data（資料）　　　　crisis —— crises（危機）

## 動詞 have

🎧 0502.mp3

| | |
|---|---|
| Do you have any sisters ╱? | 你有姊妹嗎？ |
| Yes ╲, I do ╲. | 我有。 |
| No ╲, I do not ╲. | 我沒有。 |
| No ╲, I don't ╲. | 我沒有。 |
| Does he have any brothers ╱? | 他有兄弟嗎？ |
| Yes ╲, he does ╲. | 他有。 |

| | |
|---|---|
| No ↘ , he doesn't ↘ . | 他沒有。 |
| Do they have any children ↗ ? | 他們有孩子嗎？ |
| Yes ↘ , they do ↘ . | 他們有。 |
| They have three children ↘ . | 他們有三個孩子。 |

have 作為動詞，表示 "有" 的意思，其形式跟隨人稱的變化而有所不同。I，you，we，they 用 have；he；she，it 用 has。變為疑問句的時候，要把助動詞 do 加在句首，然後把主語及動詞的位置互換：

| | |
|---|---|
| I have a bicycle. | 我有一輛單車。 |
| Do you have a bicycle? | 你有一輛單車嗎？ |

回答的時候，可以用簡略答語：Yes, I do、No, I don't。Don't 為 do not 的縮寫。如果講及第三人稱單數的時候，助動詞 do 要變為 does 的形式，而 has 則要轉為 have。

| | |
|---|---|
| She has a dictionary. | 她有一本字典。 |
| Does she have a dictionary? | 她有一本字典嗎？ |

have 除了用作動詞外，還可以用作助動詞，見下例：

| | |
|---|---|
| I have a book. | 我有一本書。 |
| I have bought a book. | 我買了一本書。 |

第 1 句的 have 為動詞，但第 2 句的 have，不表示 "有" 的意思，它只是幫助另一個動詞 bought 構成完成時態（perfect tense），所以在句子裏有助動詞的作用。

請把左右兩欄片語拼成完整句子。

🎧 0503.mp3

| | |
|---|---|
| There're four | pencils |
| Are there five | cars |
| There're six | men |
| There aren't seven | women |
| | children |

+

**There're four**

1. There're four pencils.
2. There're four cars.
3. There're four men.
4. There're four women.
5. There're four children.

**Are there five**

6. Are there five pencils?
7. Are there five cars?
8. Are there five men?
9. Are there five women?
10. Are there five children?

**There're six**

11. There're six pencils.
12. There're six cars.
13. There're six men.
14. There're six women.
15. There're six children.

**There aren't**

16. There aren't seven pencils.
17. There aren't seven cars.
18. There aren't seven men.
19. There aren't seven women.
20. There aren't seven children.

0504.mp3

| | |
|---|---|
| This coat is new. | 這件大衣是新的。 |
| These coats are new. | 這些大衣是新的。 |
| This bus is full. | 這輛巴士滿了。 |
| These buses are full. | 這些巴士都滿了。 |
| This man is old. | 這個男人年紀大了。 |
| These men are old. | 這些男人年紀都大了。 |
| This woman is young. | 這個女子很年輕。 |
| These women are young. | 這些女子都很年輕。 |
| This child is lovely. | 這個小孩子很可愛。 |
| These children are lovely. | 這些小孩子都很可愛。 |
| That street is narrow. | 那條街道很狹窄。 |
| Those streets are narrow. | 那些街道很狹窄。 |
| That building is tall. | 那座建築物很高。 |
| Those buildings are tall. | 那些建築物都很高。 |
| That house is empty. | 那所房子是空的。 |
| Those houses are empty. | 那些房子是空的。 |
| That car is old. | 那輛車是舊的。 |
| Those cars are old. | 那些車是舊的。 |

# CHAPTER 06

## I play basketball

我打籃球

**本課目標**

學會運用"現在時態"表示習慣或
真理，並以形容詞指定頻率

## 現在時態：表示動作慣性 / 恆久 / 重覆

🎧 0601.mp3

| | |
|---|---|
| I play basketball ＼ . | 我打籃球。 |
| You play tennis ＼ . | 你打網球。 |
| He plays baseball ＼ . | 他打棒球。 |
| They play badminton ＼ . | 他們打羽毛球。 |
| We play football ＼ . | 我們踢足球。 |

本課主要介紹動詞的現在時態（simple present tense）。現在時態可用於表示一個習慣的、永久的或反覆的動作，例如：

| | |
|---|---|
| He goes to school every day. | 他每天都上學。 |
| I often go to the cinema. | 我常常看電影。 |
| She sings very well. | 她唱歌唱得很好。 |
| They always go to swim. | 他們經常去游泳。 |

現在時態又可以用來表示一個普遍的事實：

| | |
|---|---|
| The sun rises in the east. | 太陽從東方升起。 |
| There are seven days in a week. | 一星期有七天。 |

要特別注意第三人稱單數動詞字尾的變化，即在動詞字尾上加上 -s 或 -es，至於其他的人稱，動詞形式並無變化。

## 頻率形容詞：表示動作的頻密程度

🎧 0602.mp3

| | |
|---|---|
| Do you often play tennis ↗? | 你常常打網球嗎？ |
| Yes ↘, I often do ↘. | 是的，我常常打的。 |
| Yes ↘, we often do ↘. | 是的，我們常常打的。 |
| Does she always play badminton ↗? | 她經常打羽毛球嗎？ |
| Yes ↘, she always does ↘. | 是的，她經常打的。 |
| No ↘, she doesn't ↘. | 不，她不打的。 |
| She never plays badminton ↘. | 她從來不打羽毛球的。 |
| She plays basketball ↘. | 她打籃球。 |

在現在時態的句子裏，我們常常見到every day（每天），always（總是），usually（通常），often（常常），sometimes（不時），never（未曾）等表示動作的頻密程度的字：

| | |
|---|---|
| Do you ever play tennis? | 你打過網球沒有？ |
| Yes, I always play tennis.<br>（Yes, I always do.） | 有，我經常打網球的。 |
| Yes, I sometimes play tennis.<br>（Yes, I sometimes do.） | 有，我有時打網球。 |
| No, I never play tennis. | 沒有，我從未打過網球。 |

# 句型練習

請把左右兩欄片語拼成完整句子。

🎧 0603 mp3

| | | |
|---|---|---|
| Are you | | a teacher of English |
| I'm not | | a student of this school |
| Is he | + | a high school student |
| He isn't | | a university student |
| She is | | a university graduate |

### Are you

❶ Are you a teacher of English?
❷ Are you a student of this school?
❸ Are you a high school student?
❹ Are you a university student?
❺ Are you a university graduate?

### I'm not

❻ I'm not a teacher of English.
❼ I'm not a student of this school.
❽ I'm not a high school student.
❾ I'm not a university student.
❿ I'm not a university graduate.

### Is he

⓫ Is he a teacher of English?
⓬ Is he a student of this school?
⓭ Is he a high school student?
⓮ Is he a university student?
⓯ Is he a university graduate?

### He isn't

⓰ He isn't a teacher of English.
⓱ He isn't a student of this school.
⓲ He isn't a high school student.
⓳ He isn't a university student.
⓴ He isn't a university graduate.

### She is

㉑ She is a teacher of English.
㉒ She is a student of this school.
㉓ She is a high school student.
㉔ She is a university student.
㉕ She is a university graduate.

# Exercise 1

請回答下列問題：

*Example:*
*What's this? (book)*
*It's a book.*

❶ What's this? (pen)

_____

❷ What's that? (egg)

_____

❸ What is it? (table)

_____

❹ What's that? (chair)

_____

❺ What is it? (apple)

_____

# CHAPTER 07

## I'm reading a book

我在看書

**本課目標**

學會運用"現在進行時態"表示動作進行中／將會發生

## 現在進行時態：表示動作進行中 / 將會發生

🎧 0701.mp3

| | |
|---|---|
| I'm reading a book ↘ . | 我在看書。 |
| What are you doing at the moment ↘ ? | 你在做甚麼？ |
| I'm writing a letter ↘ . | 我在寫信。 |
| Are you reading a book ↗ ? | 你在看書嗎？ |
| No ↘ , I'm not ↘ . | 不，我不是。 |
| I'm writing a letter ↘ . | 我在寫信。 |
| Are you writing a letter ↗ ? | 你在寫信嗎？ |
| Yes ↘ , I am ↘ . | 是的，我是。 |
| What's he doing now ↘ ? | 他在做甚麼？ |
| He's sleeping ↘ . | 他在睡覺。 |
| Is he sleeping ↗ ? | 他在睡覺嗎？ |
| Yes ↘ , he is ↘ . | 是的，他是。 |
| No ↘ , he isn't ↘ . | 不是，他不是。 |

本課主要介紹動詞的現在進行時態（present continuous tense）的句法。現在進行時態是由動詞to be的現在式（即am，are或is）加上現在分詞（present participle，即現在式加上 -ing）而成。例如：

| | |
|---|---|
| I am swimming. | You are swimming. |
| He is swimming. | |

現在進行時態可用來表示一個還沒有完成的動作，即現在還在進行中的動作。例如：

| | |
|---|---|
| We are working on the report. | 我們正在寫報告。 |
| She is playing the piano. | 她在彈鋼琴。 |

現在進行時態又可以表示將來發生的動作，通常用於 go，come，stay，leave，start 等表示動作的動詞。例如：

| | |
|---|---|
| He is coming to see you tonight. | 他今晚要來看你。 |
| They are going to Paris next Friday. | 他們下星期五到法國去。 |

請把左右兩欄片語拼成完整句子。

🎧 0702.mp3

| | | |
|---|---|---|
| Is Mr. Wong | | a Chinese |
| He is | | an engineer |
| He isn't | + | a doctor |
| Is she | | an American |
| She isn't | | an Italian |

**Is Mr. Wong**

① Is Mr. Wang a Chinese?
② Is Mr. Wang an engineer?
③ Is Mr. Wang a doctor?
④ Is Mr. Wang an American?
⑤ Is Mr. Wang an Italian?

**He is**

⑥ He is a Chinese.
⑦ He is an engineer.
⑧ He is a doctor.
⑨ He is an American.
⑩ He is an Italian.

**He isn't**

⑪ He isn't a Chinese.
⑫ He isn't an engineer.
⑬ He isn't a doctor.
⑭ He isn't an American.
⑮ He isn't an Italian.

**Is she**

⑯ Is she a chinese?
⑰ Is she an engineer?
⑱ Is she a doctor?
⑲ Is she an American?
⑳ Is she an Italian?

**She isn't**

㉑ She isn't a Chinese.
㉒ She isn't an engineer.
㉓ She isn't a doctor.
㉔ She isn't an American.
㉕ She isn't an Italian.

# Exercise 2

請回答下列問題：

*Example:*

*Is this a book? (Yes)*

*Yes, it is.*

**❶** Is this a box? (Yes)

_____

**❷** Is that an ant? (No)

_____

**❸** Is it a knife? (No)

_____

**❹** Is that a cup? (Yes)

_____

**❺** Is it a dog? (No)

_____

# CHAPTER 08

## I was a teacher two years ago

兩年前我是教師

**本課目標**

學會運用 " 過去時態 " 表示動作
完成了，或詢問動作是否完成了

# 文法及用法分析

## 過去時態：表示動作在某段期間完成了

🎧 0801.mp3

| | |
|---|---|
| I was a teacher two years ago ↘ . | 我兩年前是（一位）教師。 |
| You were a student then ↘ . | 那個時候你是（一個）學生。 |
| She wasn't a nurse ↘ . | 她不是（一位）護士。（指過去，此節以下各句都是這樣。） |

本課介紹動詞的過去時態（past tense）的句法。

過去時態表示過去某一個時間或某一段期間內完成的動作，例如：

| | |
|---|---|
| I went there a few days ago. | 我前幾天到了那裏去。 |
| The baby cried all night. | 那嬰兒哭了整個晚上。 |

過去時態的句子常常帶有 yesterday，last，this，ago 等表示時間的詞：

| | |
|---|---|
| He went to town yesterday. | 他昨天進城去了。 |
| She visited her friend last week. | 她上一個星期探望了她的朋友。 |
| I was late this morning. | 今天早上我遲到了。 |
| He lent the book to me ten days ago. | 他十天前把這本書借給了我。 |

另外一些常見的短語為：last night（昨晚），last month（上個月），last year（去年），yesterday morning（昨天早上），yesterday afternoon（昨天下午），yesterday evening（昨天晚上）。

## 動詞 be 的過去式：was, were

0802.mp3

| | |
|---|---|
| Were they doctors ╱ ? | 他們是醫生嗎？ |
| Yes ╲ , they were ╲ . | 是的，他們是。 |
| No ╲ , they weren't ╲ . | 不，他們不是。 |

2．動詞 be 的過去式為 was，were。第一人稱單數和第三人稱單數用 was，其餘的用 were。動詞 have 的過去式為 had，沒有人稱和數的變化。至於其他的動詞，一般都是在詞尾加上 -ed，如

work —— worked（工作）     play —— played（玩）

等等。

但英語裏有很多不規則動詞，其過去式的變化方法很不規則，例如

| | |
|---|---|
| go —— went（去） | come —— came（來） |
| eat —— ate（吃） | drink —— drank（喝） |
| make —— made（做） | stand —— stood（站立） |
| write —— wrote（寫） | leave —— left（離開） |
| give —— gave（給） | hear —— heard（聽見） |
| speak —— spoke（講） | meet —— met（遇見） |

……等。

Ch08

77

## 過去時態的疑問句

🎧 0003.mp3

| | |
|---|---|
| What did he do yesterday ↘ ? | 他昨天做甚麼呢？ |
| He went to the park ↘ . | 他到公園去了。 |
| Did he go to the park ↗ ? | 他到公園去了嗎？ |
| Yes ↘ , he did ↘ . | 是的，他去了。 |
| No ↘ , he didn't ↘ . | 不，他沒去。 |
| I lived in England last year ↘ . | 去年我住在英國。 |
| Did you live in England last year ↗ ? | 去年你住在英國嗎？ |
| Yes ↘ , I did ↘ . | 是的，我是。 |

把過去時態的句型轉為疑問句，要用助動詞 do 的過去式 did，而句子裏的動詞要變為現在式。例如：

| | |
|---|---|
| He stayed at home last night. | 他昨晚留在家裏。 |
| Did he stay at home last night? | 他昨晚有沒有留在家裏？ |
| She left Hong Kong two years ago. | 她兩年前離開了香港。 |
| Did she leave Hong Kong two years ago? | 她兩年前離開了香港嗎？ |

# 句型練習

請把左右兩欄片語拼成完整句子。

🎧 0804.mp3

| | | |
|---|---|---|
| Were you out | | last night |
| I was in | | all evening |
| You were busy | + | this evening |
| Were you ill | | last Sunday |
| | | yesterday morning |

**Were you out**

① Were you out last night?
② Were you out all evening?
③ Were you out this evening?
④ Were you out last Sunday?
⑤ Were you out yesterday morning?

**I was in**

⑥ I was in last night.
⑦ I was in all evening.
⑧ I was in this evening.
⑨ I was in last Sunday.
⑩ I was in yesterday morning.

**You were busy**

⑪ You were busy last night.
⑫ You were busy all evening.
⑬ You were busy this evening.
⑭ You were busy last Sunday.
⑮ You were busy yesterday morning.

**Were you ill**

⑯ Were you ill last night?
⑰ Were you ill all evening?
⑱ Were you ill this evening?
⑲ Were you ill last Sunday?
⑳ Were you ill yesterday morning?

請把左右兩欄片語拼成完整句子。

🎧 0805 mp3

| | |
|---|---|
| I wrote two letters | yesterday |
| I read the magazine | last night |
| I sat up till late | + the other day |
| I heard him sing | the night before last |
| | five days ago |

### I wrote two letters

❶ I wrote two letters yesterday.

❷ I wrote two letters last night.

❸ I wrote two letters the other day.

❹ I wrote two letters the night before last.

❺ I wrote two letters five days ago.

### I read the magazine

❻ I read the magazine yesterday.

❼ I read the magazine last night.

❽ I read the magazine the other day.

❾ I read the magazine the night before last.

❿ I read the magazine five days ago.

### I sat up till late

⓫ I sat up till late yesterday.

⓬ I sat up till late last night.

⓭ I sat up till late the other day.

⓮ I sat up till late the night before last.

⓯ I sat up till late five days ago.

### I heard him sing

⓰ I heard him sing yesterday.

⓱ I heard him sing last night.

⓲ I heard him sing the other day.

⓳ I heard him sing the night before last.

⓴ I heard him sing five days ago.

請依照例子造句:

*Example:*

I am a teacher. (You)

You are a teacher.

❶ I'm a doctor. (You)

_____

❷ I'm a nurse. (She)

_____

❸ You're a clerk. (He)

_____

❹ We're students. (They)

_____

❺ I'm a boy. (We)

_____

# CHAPTER 09

## I shall go on picnic tommorrow

### 明天我去旅行

**本課目標**

學會運用"將來時態"表示動作
將會發生，以及提出請示或請求

# 文法及用法分析

## 將來時態

| | |
|---|---|
| I shall go on a picnic tomorrow ＼. | 明天我去旅行。 |
| You'll be twenty years old next year ＼. | 明年你二十歲了。 |
| He'll visit you soon ＼. | 他不久就會探望你的。 |
| They won't sell the house ＼. | 他們不會賣掉房子。 |
| We shall go to the cinema ＼. | 我們會去看電影。 |

將來時態（future tense）表示將來某一時刻或將來經常的動作或狀態。將來式由助動詞shall或will，加上不帶to的動詞不定式（infinitive without "to"）構成。第一人稱用shall，第二、三人稱則用will。但美國英語則不管甚麼人稱，一律都用will。

| | |
|---|---|
| We shall see him tomorrow. | 我們明天見他。 |
| He will start working next week. | 他下個星期開始工作。 |
| She will be in London in a few days. | 她幾天後就會到倫敦來。 |

將來式常常與一些表示將來的詞連用，例如

| | |
|---|---|
| tomorrow（明天） | next week（下星期） |
| from now on（從現在開始） | in a month（一個月後） |
| in the future（將來） | soon（不久） |

## 以 shall 表示強烈意願

shall用於第一人稱表示將來時態，但用於第二及第三人稱時則表示說話者的"意願"、"決心"、"允諾"或"威脅"等等。例如：

| He shall not enter my house again. | 我不准他再來我家。 |
| You shall do it all over again. | 你要重新再做一次。 |
| All members shall pay a subscription of ten dollars per year. | 所有會員每年都要付十塊錢會費。 |
| You shall have an ice-cream if you do your homework. | 如果你做功課，給你雪糕吃。 |
| He shall be punished if he behaves badly. | 如果他不守規矩，他就要受罰。 |

## 以 shall 表示請示

🎧 0902.mp3

| Shall we go to the cinema ↗? | 我們去看電影好嗎？ |
| I'll come to the party ↘. | 我一定會參加聚會的。 |
| Shall I open the window ↗? | 我可以把窗子打開嗎？ |

shall 用於疑問句中之第一人稱及第三人稱，表示“請示”之意，即詢問被問者的意願。例如：

| Shall I turn on the radio? | 你要我把收音機打開嗎？ |
| Shall the boy wait? | 你要那孩子等待嗎？ |

will 用於第二及第三人稱表示將來時態，如果用於第一人稱，則表示說話者的“意願”、“決心”或“應允”：

| I will come tomorrow. | 我明天一定會來。 |
| I won't(will not)do it again. | 我不會再做那事情了。 |
| We'll help you. | 我們會幫助你。 |
| I won't see you again. | 我不想再見你。 |

## 以 shall 表示請求

0903.mp3

| | |
|---|---|
| Will you come here, please ╱ ? | 請你過這邊來好嗎? |
| He'll do it ╲ . | 他會這樣做。 |

will 用於疑問句中之第二人稱,表示 "請求" 之意:

| | |
|---|---|
| Will you come in? | 請你進來好嗎? |
| Will you open the window? | 請你把窗子打開好嗎? |

## 以 going to 表示將發生的事

0904.mp3

要表示即將發生的事,也可以用以下的句型:

| | |
|---|---|
| It is going to rain. | 快要下雨了。 |
| I'm going to tell you a story. | 我就要給你們講一個故事。 |

上述句型的結構為 to be going 加上帶 to 的動詞不定式 (infinitive with "to")。這種句型在口語中較為常用。

# 句型練習

請把左右兩欄片語拼成完整句子。

🎧 0905.mp3

| | | |
|---|---|---|
| She'll be | | out this afternoon |
| Will you be | | in all day today |
| I'll be | + | present this morning |
| Will he be | | absent tomorrow |
| | | at your house |

### She'll be

① She'll be out this afternoon.
② She'll be in all day today.
③ She'll be present this morning.
④ She'll be absent tomorrow.
⑤ She'll be at your house.

### Will you be

⑥ Will you be out this afternoon?
⑦ Will you be in all day today?
⑧ Will you be present this morning?
⑨ Will you be absent tomorrow?
⑩ Will you be at your house?

### I'll be

⑪ I'll be out this afternoon.
⑫ I'll be in all day today.
⑬ I'll be present this morning.
⑭ I'll be absent tomorrow.
⑮ I'll be at your house.

### Will he be

⑯ Will he be out this afternoon?
⑰ Will he be in all day today?
⑱ Will he be present this morning?
⑲ Will he be absent tomorrow?
⑳ Will he be at your house?

87

請把左右兩欄片語拼成完整句子。

0906 mp3

| | |
|---|---|
| Will you go out | this evening |
| I won't go out | today |
| I'll stay at home | + tomorrow |
| Will you visit him | tomorrow evening |
| I won't go there | |

### Will you go out

1. Will you go out this evening?
2. Will you go out today?
3. Will you go out tomorrow?
4. Will you go out tomorrow evening?

### I won't go out

5. I won't go out this evening.
6. I won't go out today.
7. I won't go out tomorrow.
8. I won't go out tomorrow evening.

### I'll stay at home

9. I'll stay at home this evening.
10. I'll stay at home today.
11. I'll stay at home tomorrow.
12. I'll stay at home tomorrow evening.

### Will you visit him

13. Will you visit him this evening?
14. Will you visit him today?
15. Will you visit him tomorrow?
16. Will you visit him tomorrow evening?

### I won't go there

17. I won't go there this evening.
18. I won't go there today.
19. I won't go there tomorrow.
20. I won't go there tomorrow evening.

# Exercise 4

把下列句子轉為疑問句：

① I am a boy.

_____

② She is a girl.

_____

③ We are doctors.

_____

④ I am Tom.

_____

⑤ They are teachers.

_____

# CHAPTER 10

## I have just finished my homework

我剛剛做好功課

**本課目標**

學會運用"現在完成時態"表示
動作剛完成或未完成的動作

# 文法及用法分析

## 現在完成時態表達形式

🎧 1001.mp3

| | |
|---|---|
| I have just finished my homework ↘. | 我剛剛做完功課。 |
| Has he finished his homework ↗? | 他做完了功課沒有？ |
| Yes ↘, he has ↘. | 他做完了。 |
| No ↘, he hasn't finished yet ↘. | 他還沒有做完。 |

現在完成時態（present perfect tense）由 to have 的現在式加上過去分詞（past participle）而成：

| | |
|---|---|
| I have worked. | You have worked. |
| He has worked. | We have worked. |
| They have worked. | |

規則動詞的過去分詞和過去式的形式一樣，例如 walk 和 work 的過去分詞為 walked 和 worked；但不規則動詞的過去分詞變化很不劃一，以下是常見的例子：

| | |
|---|---|
| come —— come | be —— been |
| begin —— begun | bring —— brought |
| buy —— bought | catch —— caught |
| drink —— drunk | eat —— eaten |
| give —— given | go —— gone |
| have —— had | leave —— left |
| make —— made | run —— run |
| see —— seen | take —— taken |
| teach —— taught | write —— written |

## 現在完成時態的三種含意

1002.mp3

| | |
|---|---|
| He has just gone out ↘ . | 他剛剛出去了。 |
| She has lived in Hong Kong for ten years ↘ . | 她住在香港已經十年了。 |
| She has taught in this school since last year ↘ . | 去年開始她已經在這家學校任教。 |
| Have you had lunch ↗ ? | 你吃過了午飯沒有？ |
| Yes ↘ , I had it at twelve o'clock ↘ . | 吃過了，我十二點鐘吃的。 |
| No ↘ , I haven't had it yet ↘ . | 還沒有。 |
| Have you ever been to London ↗ ? | 你到過倫敦沒有？ |
| Yes ↘ , I have ↘ . | 我到過。 |
| No ↘ , I've never been to London ↘ . | 我沒有到過倫敦。 |

現在完成時態可以用於表示一個剛剛完成的動作，例如：

| | |
|---|---|
| He has just gone out. | 他剛剛出去了。 |
| I have just finished reading the book. | 我剛剛把那本書看完。 |

現在完成時態又可以用於表示過去的動作，但這動作沒有確定的時間：

| | |
|---|---|
| I haven't seen him recently. | 我近來沒有見過他。 |
| Have you had breakfast? | 你吃過了早餐沒有？ |

現在完成時態亦可以用於表示一個開始於過去而延續到現在的動作：

| | |
|---|---|
| I have been in Hong Kong for three months. | 我住在香港已經三個月了。 |
| He has lived in Canada since last year. | 自去年開始，他便住在加拿大。 |

# 句型練習

請把左右兩欄片語拼成完整句子。

🎧 1003.mp3

| | | |
|---|---|---|
| I often | | call on my friends |
| Sometimes I | | play tennis |
| In the morning I | + | go to the cinema |
| In the afternoon I | | go on a picnic |
| | | review English lessons |

I often

1. I often call on my friends.
2. I often play tennis.
3. I often go to the cinema.
4. I often go on a picnic.
5. I often review English lessons.

Sometimes I

6. Sometimes I call on my friends.
7. Sometimes I play tennis.
8. Sometimes I go to the cinema.
9. Sometimes I go on a picnic.
10. Sometimes I review English lessons.

In the morning I

11. In the morning I call on my friends.
12. In the morning I play tennis.
13. In the morning I go to the cinema.
14. In the morning I go on a picnic.
15. In the morning I review English lessons.

In the afternoon I

16. In the afternoon I call on my friends.
17. In the afternoon I play tennis.
18. In the afternoon I go to the cinema.
19. In the afternoon I go on a picnic.
20. In the afternoon I review English lessons.

# Exercise 5

請回答下列問題：

*Example:*

Are you a doctor? (Yes)

Yes, I am.

① Are you a student? (Yes)

_____

② Are you a nurse? (No)

_____

③ Is he a teacher? (No)

_____

④ Am I a worker? (Yes)

_____

⑤ Are they clerks? (Yes)

_____

# CHAPTER 11

## I can speak English

### 我會説英語

**本課目標**

學會運用 " 助動詞 " can、 must、may

# 文法及用法分析

## can= 能力

🎧 1101.mp3

| | |
|---|---|
| I can speak English ﹨. | 我會説英語。 |
| Can you speak German ／? | 你會説德文嗎？ |
| Yes ﹨, I can ﹨. | 是的，我會。 |
| No ﹨, I can't ﹨. | 不，我不會。 |
| Can he play the guitar ／? | 他會玩結他嗎？ |
| No ﹨, he can't ﹨. | 不，他不會。 |

本課主要介紹助動詞can，must，may等的用法。助動詞本身的意思並不完整，要和一般的動詞一起用才能構成完整的意思。助動詞can表示能力，例如：

| | |
|---|---|
| Can you drive a car? | 你能開汽車嗎？ |
| I can play the piano. | 我會彈鋼琴。 |

can用於疑問句及否定句，表示説話者的"懷疑"、"猜測"或"不肯定"，例如：

| | |
|---|---|
| Where can they be? | 他們會在甚麼地方呢？ |
| He cannot be so careless. | 他不可能這麼大意的。 |

在口語中，can可以代替may，表示"許可"的意思：

| | |
|---|---|
| You can drop in anytime. | 你隨時都可以來。 |
| Can I borrow your book? | 可以把你的書借給我嗎？ |

can的過去式是could。其他的時態都要用be able to來表示：

| | |
|---|---|
| He will be able to come on Friday. | 他星期五可以來。 |
| We shall be able to finish the work next month. | 我們下個月就可以把工作做完了。 |

## must= 必須

| | |
|---|---|
| I must go ↘. | 我得走了。 |
| Must you go so soon ↗? | 你那麼快就走嗎？ |
| Yes ↘, I must ↘. | 是的，我一定要。 |
| No ↘, I needn't ↘. | 不，我不必這樣做。 |

must 表示"應當"或"必須"的意思：

| | |
|---|---|
| You must be punctual. | 你必須準時。 |
| We must observe the rules. | 我們應該遵守規則。 |

must 的否定式有"禁止"的意思：

| | |
|---|---|
| You must not go in. | 你不可以進去。 |
| You must not park your car here. | 你不可把你的汽車停放在這。 |

如果要表示"不必"的意思，就要用 need not：

| | |
|---|---|
| Must we hand in the Exercise today? | 我們必須今天交練習嗎？ |
| No, you need not. | 不，不必交。 |

must 沒有過去式，如果要表示其他的時態，就要用 have to（必須）：

| | |
|---|---|
| We will have to get up very early tomorrow. | 我們明天必須起得很早。 |
| At that time, she had to work very hard. | 那時候她不得不努力工作。 |
| He has to go to school every day. | 他每天必須上學。 |

注意口語中的 I have got to = I have to, you have got to = you have to ... 。

99

## may= 可能

1103.mp3

| | |
|---|---|
| I may not come tomorrow ↘. | 明天我可能不來。 |
| May I come in ↘? | 我可以進來嗎？ |

may表示說話的人的猜測，認為某一事“或許”或“可能”發生：

| | |
|---|---|
| He may know the name of that girl. | 他可能知道那個女孩子的名字。 |
| She may not go to the concert. | 她可能不去音樂會了。 |

may又可以表示允許或請求：

| | |
|---|---|
| You may go now. | 你現在可以走了。 |
| May I see your identity card? | 我可以看看你的身份證嗎？ |

# 句型練習

請把左右兩欄片語拼成完整句子。

🎧 1104.mp3

| Can you | | speak French |
|---------|---|--------------|
| I can | + | come at noon |
| You can't | | answer easy questions |
| Can't you | | understand it |

## Can you

❶ Can you speak French?
❷ Can you come at noon?
❸ Can you answer easy questions?
❹ Can you understand it?

## I can

❺ I can speak French.
❻ I can come at noon.
❼ I can answer easy questions.
❽ I can understand it.

## You can't

❾ You can't speak French.
❿ You can't come at noon.
⓫ You can't answer easy questions.
⓬ You can't understand it.

## Can't you

⓭ Can't you speak French?
⓮ Can't you come at noon?
⓯ Can't you answer easy questions?
⓰ Can't you understand it?

請把左右兩欄片語拼成完整句子。

1105 mp3

| You must | go to the post office |
| Must you | drop it in a mailbox |
| I must | send it by express delivery |
| He must | register this letter |

+

## You must

1. You must go to the post office.
2. You must drop it in a mailbox.
3. You must send it by express delivery.
4. You must register this letter.

## Must you

5. Must you go to the post office?
6. Must you drop it in a mailbox?
7. Must you send it by express delivery?
8. Must you register this letter?

## I must

9. I must go to the post office.
10. I must drop it in a mailbox.
11. I must send it by express delivery.
12. I must register this letter.

## He must

13. He must go to the post office.
14. He must drop it in a mailbox.
15. He must send it by express delivery.
16. He must register this letter.

# Exercise 6

請依照例子造句：

*Example:*

*This pen belongs to you.*

*It's your pen.*

① This book belongs to me.

_____

② That pencil belongs to Tom.

_____

③ This coat belongs to my sister.

_____

④ That car belongs to us.

_____

⑤ This house belongs to them.

_____

# CHAPTER 12

## You ought to do your homework

你應該做功課

**本課目標**

學會運用〝助動詞〞ought、dare

# 文法及用法分析

## ought = 應該

🎵 1201.mp3

| | |
|---|---|
| You ought to do your homework ↘. | 你應該做功課。 |
| Ought we to do it at once ↗? | 我們應該立刻去做嗎？ |
| You ought to do it tomorrow ↘. | 你應該明天去做。 |
| He ought to pay the debt ↘. | 他該還債。 |

ought 表示義務、責任或規勸，但語氣沒有 must 和 have to 那麼重。ought 沒有時態、人稱和數的變化，可以用於現在、過去或將來時態，ought 之後的動詞要用帶 "to" 的動詞不定式：

| | |
|---|---|
| You ought to go there. | 你應當到那裏去。 |
| She ought to get up earlier. | 她該早點起床。 |

ought 有時又可以表示猜測：

| | |
|---|---|
| He ought to arrive now. | 他現在該到了。 |
| She ought to be in the canteen. | 她想必在飯堂裏。 |

ought 後接完成時態的不定式（perfect infinitive），表示該做而事實上沒有做的事情：

| | |
|---|---|
| You ought to have told me before. | 你該早點告訴我。 |
| He ought to have taken the medicine. | 他早就該吃藥了。 |

ought 的否定式是 ought not（oughtn't），疑問句的形式是 Ought I...? Ought you ...? Ought he...?

## dare = 敢

🎧 1202.mp3

| | |
|---|---|
| He dare not jump into the river ＼. | 他不敢跳進河裏去。 |
| Dare you jump into the river ／? | 你敢跳進河裏去嗎？ |
| No ＼, I dare not do it ＼. | 不，我不敢做。 |
| They dared not move ＼. | 他們不敢動。 |
| Dared he go ／? | 他敢去嗎？ |

在肯定句子，dare 的作用就像普通動詞一樣，但在疑問句及否定句中，dare 則可以用作普通動詞或助動詞。現在看看 dare 作為助動詞的用法：

| | |
|---|---|
| I dare not open the door. | 我不敢開門。 |
| She dared not climb up the ladder. | 她不敢爬上梯子去。 |
| Dare you go to see him? | 你敢去見他嗎？ |
| Dared he kill the cat? | 他敢殺死貓嗎？ |

dared 為 dare 的過去式。

請把左右兩欄片語拼成完整句子。

🎧 1203.mp3

| May I | | send this by parcel post |
|---|---|---|
| You may | | try this on |
| You must | + | write your name here |
| You mustn't | | hang this on a coat hanger |

### May I

❶ May I send this by parcel post?
❷ May I try this on?
❸ May I write your name here?
❹ May I hang this on a coat hanger?

### You may

❺ You may send this by parcel post.
❻ You may try this on.
❼ You may write your name here.
❽ You may hang his on a coat hanger.

### You must

❾ You must send this by parcel post.
❿ You must try this on.
⓫ You must write your name here.
⓬ You must hang this on a coat hanger.

### You mustn't

⓭ You mustn't send this by parcel post.
⓮ You mustn't try this on.
⓯ You mustn't write your name here.
⓰ You mustn't hang this on a coat hanger.

請把左右兩欄片語拼成完整句子。

🎧 1204.mp3

| You ought to | be more careful |
|---|---|
| I ought to | take a few days off |
| He ought to | + pay more attention |
| You had better | take a rest |

**You ought to**
1. You ought to be more careful.
2. You ought to take a few days off.
3. You ought to pay more attention.
4. You ought to take a rest.

**I ought to**
5. I ought to be more careful.
6. I ought to take a few days off.
7. I ought to pay more attention.
8. I ought to take a rest.

**He ought to**
9. He ought to be more careful.
10. He ought to take a few days off.
11. He ought to pay more attention.
12. He ought to take a rest.

**You had better**
13. You had better be more careful.
14. You had better take a few days off.
15. You had better pay more attention.
16. You had better take a rest.

# Exercise 7

請依照例子造句：

*Example:*

This is my book.

It's mine.

**1** This is their house.

_____

**2** That's his pencil.

_____

**3** That's our car.

_____

**4** This is your pen.

_____

**5** This is my sister's coat.

_____

# CHAPTER 13

**I've been waiting for you for an hour**

我等了你一個小時了

## 本課目標

學會運用三種時態：
① 現在完成進行時態
② 將來進行時態
③ 將來完成時態

## 現在完成進行時態

🎧 1301.mp3

| | |
|---|---|
| I've been waiting for you for an hour ↘. | 我等了你一個小時了。 |
| Have you been waiting long ↗? | 你等了很久嗎？ |
| He has been studying since early morning ↘. | 他從清早開始，就一直在溫習。 |
| I've been writing letters since seven o'clock ↘. | 我從七點鐘開始，就一直在寫信。 |

本課介紹三種時態，其中一種為現在完成進行時態（present perfect continuous tense），其形式是動詞 "to be" 的完成式，加上現在分詞（present participle），例如：I have been sleeping, she has been sleeping....。

現在完成進行時態可以表示從過去某一時刻一直延續到現在的動作：

| | |
|---|---|
| She has been living here for two months. | 她在這兒住了兩個月了。 |
| I have been learning German for three years. | 我學德文已經有三年了。 |

現在完成進行時態又可以表示反覆進行的動作：

| | |
|---|---|
| His mother has been thinking of him all the time. | 他媽媽一直在想念他。 |
| I have been looking for him all morning. | 我整個早上一直在找他。 |

## 將來進行時態

🎧 1302.mp3

| | |
|---|---|
| She'll be taking her examination next week ↘. | 她下個星期就要參加考試。 |
| He'll be reading my letter tomorrow night ↘. | 他明天晚上就會看到我的信。 |
| I shall be studying in the library tomorrow afternoon ↘. | 明天下午我將會在圖書館裏溫習。 |

將來進行時態（future continuous tense）的形式是動詞 "to be" 的將來式，加上現在分詞，例如：I shall be working, she will be working...。

將來進行時態表示將來某一時刻或某一段時間正在進行的動作；常和表示將來的時間副詞一起用。例如：

| | |
|---|---|
| I'll be taking my French lessons tomorrow evening. | 明天晚上我要上法文課。 |

## 將來完成時態

🎧 1303.mp3

| | |
|---|---|
| By June I shall have finished writing the book ↘. | 到六月的時候，我就會把這本書寫完。 |
| He shall have gone to Japan by Monday ↘. | 到星期一的時候，他已經到日本去了。 |

**Ch13**

將來完成時態（future perfect tense）的形式是 shall have 或者 will have，加上過去分詞（past participle），例如：I shall have worked, he will have worked... 。

將來完成時態用於表示將來某時間以前已經完成的動作：

| | |
|---|---|
| By the end of July I shall have finished my secondary school course. | 到七月底的時候，我就會完成我的中學課程。 |
| By the time you come back, he will have left Hong Kong. | 到你回來的時候，他將已離開香港了。 |

# 句型練習

請把左右兩欄片語拼成完整句子。

🎧 1304.mp3

| It's cold in | | November |
|---|---|---|
| Is it warm in | | December |
| Does it snow in | + | winter |
| It doesn't rain in | | spring |
| | | January |

It's cold in

❶ It's cold in November.
❷ It's cold in December.
❸ It's cold in winter.
❹ It's cold in spring.
❺ It's cold in January.

Is it warm in

❻ Is it warm in November?
❼ Is it warm in December?
❽ Is it warm in winter?
❾ Is it warm in spring?
❿ Is it warm in January?

Does it snow in

⓫ Does it snow in November?
⓬ Does it snow in December?
⓭ Does it snow in winter?
⓮ Does it snow in spring?
⓯ Does it snow in January?

It doesn't rain in

⓰ It doesn't rain in November.
⓱ It doesn't rain in December.
⓲ It doesn't rain in winter.
⓳ It doesn't rain in spring.
⓴ It doesn't rain in January.

請把左右兩欄片語拼成完整句子。

🎧 1305.mp3

| | | |
|---|---|---|
| Do you work | | on Sundays |
| What do you do | | on Mondays |
| Do you go to school | + | on Fridays |
| I go to the cinema | | on Saturdays |
| | | on holidays |

### Do you work

❶ Do you work on Sundays?
❷ Do you work on Mondays?
❸ Do you work on Fridays?
❹ Do you work on Saturdays?
❺ Do you work on holidays?

### What do you do

❻ What do you do on Sundays?
❼ What do you do on Mondays?
❽ What do you do on Fridays?
❾ What do you do on Saturdays?
❿ What do you do on holidays?

### Do you go to school

⓫ Do you go to school on Sundays?
⓬ Do you go to school on Mondays?
⓭ Do you go to school on Fridays?
⓮ Do you go to school on Saturdays?
⓯ Do you go to school on holidays?

### I go to the cinema

⓰ I go to the cinema on Sundays.
⓱ I go to the cinema on Mondays.
⓲ I go to the cinema on Fridays.
⓳ I go to the cinema on Saturdays.
⓴ I go to the cinema on holidays.

# CHAPTER 14

## She is a clever girl

她是個機靈的女孩子

**本課目標**

學會運用 "形容詞" 修飾人或物

# 文法及用法分析

## 形容詞：修飾名詞或代名詞

🎧 1401.mp3

|  |  |
|---|---|
| She is a clever girl ↘. | 她是個聰明的女孩子。 |
| He wears a white shirt ↘. | 他穿了一件白色的襯衣。 |
| This book belongs to me ↘. | 這本書是我的。 |
| That girl is John's sister ↘. | 那個女孩子是約翰的姊姊（妹妹）。 |
| Every boy is happy ↘. | 所有的男孩子都快樂。 |
| Each student has his own book ↘. | 每一個學生都有他自己的書。 |
| Some students were absent ↘. | 有些學生缺課。 |
| Few students were present ↘. | 很少學生上課。 |
| What colour do you want ↘? | 你要甚麼顏色的？ |
| Which car is yours ↘? | 哪一輛車是你的？ |

本課主要介紹形容詞（adjectives）。形容詞在句子中有修飾名詞或代名詞的作用。形容詞分為六種：

❶ 性質形容詞（qualifying adjectives）表示人或物的性質：

| | |
|---|---|
| He is a fat man. | 他是一個胖子。 |
| The table is square. | 這張桌子是方形的。 |

❷ 數量形容詞（quantitative adjectives）包括 some、any、no、few、little、many、much、one、two、three……等詞，用來表示事物的多少。

❸ 指示形容詞（demonstrative adjectives）包括 this、that、these、those 等等，用來指出要說明的人或事物。

④ 個別形容詞（distributive adjectives）指能夠表示出個別所要說明的人或事物的形容詞，常用的有 each 和 every。

Each 和 every 的分別不大，都是指全體的人或物，但 each 可用作代名詞，而 every 卻不能；each 可用於數目小的情況下，例如兩個人；而 every 則通常用於較大的數目。

⑤ 疑問形容詞（interrogative adjectives）：what，which，whose 等字如果和名詞一起連用，而用於疑問句的話，就屬於疑問形容詞。

⑥ 所有形容詞（possessive adjectives）是能夠表示事物持有人的形容詞，例如 my，your，his，her……等等。（詳細解釋請參考第 3 課）

請把左右兩欄片語拼成完整句子。

🎧 1402.mp3

| Do you | | understand |
|---|---|---|
| I | | make mistakes |
| I don't | + | know his name |
| Does he | | teach German |
| | | read newspapers |

**Do you**

❶ Do you understand?
❷ Do you make mistakes?
❸ Do you know his name?
❹ Do you teach German?
❺ Do you read newspapers?

**I**

❻ I understand.
❼ I make mistakes.
❽ I know his name.
❾ I teach German.
❿ I read newspapers.

**I don't**

⓫ I don't understand.
⓬ I don't make mistakes.
⓭ I don't know his name.
⓮ I don't teach German.
⓯ I don't read newspapers.

**Does he**

⓰ Does he understand?
⓱ Does he make mistakes?
⓲ Does he know his name?
⓳ Does he teach German?
⓴ Does he read newspapers?

1403.mp3

| | |
|---|---|
| He's old. | 他年紀大了。 |
| He's an old man. | 他是一位老人。 |
| He's stout. | 他很強壯。 |
| He's a stout man. | 他是一條壯漢。 |
| He's young. | 他很年輕。 |
| He's a young man. | 他是一個青年。 |
| He's thin. | 他很瘦。 |
| He's a thin man. | 他是一個瘦子。 |
| She isn't old. | 她不老。 |
| She isn't an old woman. | 她不是一位老婦。 |
| She isn't young. | 她不年輕。 |
| She isn't a young woman. | 她不是一個年輕女子。 |
| She isn't thin. | 她不瘦。 |
| She isn't a thin woman. | 她不是一個瘦的女人。 |
| She isn't tall. | 她不高。 |
| She isn't a tall woman. | 她不是一個高個子的女人。 |

# CHAPTER 15

**He runs quickly**

他跑得快

**本課目標**

學會運用＂副詞＂修飾動詞、
形容詞或其他副詞

## 副詞：修飾動詞、形容詞或另一副詞

🎧 1501.mp3

| | |
|---|---|
| He runs quickly ＼. | 他跑得快。 |
| The doctor examined the patient carefully ＼. | 醫生小心地替病人檢查。 |
| The sun goes down in the west ＼. | 太陽從西方落下。 |
| Please come here ＼. | 請到這邊來。 |
| He will arrive soon ＼. | 他很快就來到。 |
| It is hot today ＼. | 今天天氣很熱。 |
| He is always late for school ＼. | 他上學經常遲到。 |
| She has been there twice ＼. | 她到過那裏兩次。 |
| The railway station is quite near ＼. | 火車站就在附近。 |
| He can hardly see the signpost ＼. | 他幾乎看不見路標。 |

本課主要介紹副詞（adverbs），其在句子中的作用為修飾動詞、形容詞或另外一個副詞。副詞共有七種：

❶ 表示狀態的副詞（adverbs of manner），例如 quickly，fast，carefully……等等。

❷ 表示地點的副詞（adverbs of place），例如 here，there，up，down……等等。

❸ 表示時間的副詞（adverbs of time），例如 soon，today，now……等等。

❹ 表示頻率的副詞（adverbs of frequency），例如 always，twice，never，often……等等。

❺ 表示程度的副詞（adverbs of degree），例如 quite，hardly，rather，fairly，too……等等。

❻ 疑問副詞（interrogative adverbs），例如 when? where? why?

❼ 關係副詞（relative adverbs），例如 when，where，why。

# 句型練習

請把左右兩欄片語拼成完整句子。

🎧 1502.mp3

| | | |
|---|---|---|
| Is he | | taking a walk |
| The man is | | wearing a suit |
| She isn't | + | wearing jeans |
| Is his wife | | sitting on a bench |
| | | walking along the road |

## Is he

1. Is he taking a walk?
2. Is he wearing a suit?
3. Is he wearing jeans?
4. Is he sitting on a bench?
5. Is he walking along the road?

## The man is

6. The man is taking a walk.
7. The man is wearing a suit.
8. The man is wearing jeans.
9. The man is sitting on a bench.
10. The man is walking along the road.

## She isn't

11. She isn't taking a walk.
12. She isn't wearing a suit.
13. She isn't wearing jeans.
14. She isn't sitting on a bench.
15. She isn't walking along the road.

## Is his wife

16. Is his wife taking a walk?
17. Is his wife wearing suit?
18. Is his wife wearing jeans?
19. Is his wife sitting on a bench?
20. Is his wife walking along the road?

125

# CHAPTER 16

## I get up at six o'clock every morning

每天清早我六點鐘起床

## 本課目標

學會運用〝前置詞〞指定時間或地點

## 以前置詞時間

🎧 1601.mp3

| | |
|---|---|
| I get up at six o'clock every morning ＼. | 我每天清早六點鐘起床。 |
| We have lunch at noon every day ＼. | 我們每天中午吃午飯。 |
| We have no school on Sundays ＼. | 我們星期天不用上學。 |
| John will leave Hong Kong on June the 3rd ＼. | 約翰會在六月三號離開香港。 |
| He will arrive here in May ＼. | 他五月就到這兒來。 |
| We went to the park early in the morning ＼. | 我們大清早就到公園去了。 |

前置詞（prepositions）放在名詞或代名詞前面，用以表示該名詞或代名詞與句子其他成分的關係。表示時間我們可以用 at, on 或 in: at 指特定的時間，例如 at two o'clock; on 指在某一天，例如 on Saturday; in 指在某一段時間，例如 in winter。

## 以前置詞指定地點

🎧 1602.mp3

| | |
|---|---|
| Please put the cup on the table ＼. | 請把茶杯放在桌子上。 |
| He lives in Hong Kong ＼. | 他住在香港。 |
| I stayed at home yesterday ＼. | 我昨天留在家裏。 |
| I live at 23 Redwood Road. | 我住在紅林道二十三號。 |

表示地點的時候，地區範圍較小的，我們可以用 at，例如 at a small village, at 10 Park Road, at a bus-stop 等等。範圍較大的，我們可以用 in，例如 in the city, in a forest, in the street。

## 前置詞 in, into

in 和 into 這兩個前置詞很容易混淆，in 表示位置，是靜態的；而 into 則是動態的，表示進入：

🎧 1603.mp3

| | |
|---|---|
| I was in the room. | 我在房間。 |
| I went into the room. | 我走進房間。 |

## 前置詞 for, since

for 和 since 用於表示時間的時候，for 用於表示某一"段"時間，而 since 則表示某一"個"時間，動作由某個時間開始，延續到說話的時候：

🎧 1604.mp3

| | |
|---|---|
| He has been here for two years. | 他在這兒已經兩年了。 |
| He has been here since 1997. | 他從一九九七年開始就在這兒了。 |

## 前置詞 between, among

between 和 among 也是很容易混淆的兩個前置詞。between 用於兩個人的情況，among 則用於兩個人以上的情況：

🎧 1605.mp3

| | |
|---|---|
| Share the apple between you. | 你們兩人平分這個蘋果。 |
| He divided his money among his sons. | 他把錢分給他的兒子們。 |

129

# 句型練習

請把左右兩欄片語拼成完整句子。

🎧 1606.mp3

| | | |
|---|---|---|
| Where did you go | | last Sunday |
| What did you do | | in the morning |
| Were you at home | + | in the evening |
| I didn't go anywhere | | yesterday |
| | | the day before yesterday |

## Where did you go

① Where did you go last Sunday?
② Where did you go in the morning?
③ Where did you go in the evening?
④ Where did you go yesterday?
⑤ Where did you go the day before yesterday?

## What did you do

⑥ What did you do last Sunday?
⑦ What did you do in the morning?
⑧ What did you do in the evening?
⑨ What did you do yesterday?
⑩ What did you do the day before yesterday?

## Were you at home

⑪ Were you at home last Sunday?
⑫ Were you at home in the morrning?
⑬ Were you at home in the evening?
⑭ Were you at home yesterday?
⑮ Were you at home the day before yesterday?

## I didn't go anywhere

⑯ I didn't go anywhere last Sunday.
⑰ I didn't go anywhere in the morning.
⑱ I didn't go anywhere in the evening.
⑲ I didn't go anywhere yesterday.
⑳ I didn't go anywhere the day before yesterday.

# 句型變化

1607.mp3

| | |
|---|---|
| the man on the right | 右邊那個人 |
| the man who is on the right | 在右邊的那個人 |
| the woman on the left | 左邊那個女人 |
| the woman who is on the left | 在左邊的那個女人 |
| the girl in the middle | 當中那個女孩子 |
| the girl who is in the middle | 在當中的那個女孩子 |
| the boy in front of me | 我前面的男孩子 |
| the boy who is in front of me | 在我前面的那個男孩子 |
| the child behind her | 她後邊的兒童 |
| the child who is behind her | 在她後邊的兒童 |
| the men in the office | 辦公室裏的男人 |
| the men who are in the office | 在辦公室裏的男人 |
| the women at church | 教堂裏的婦女 |
| the women who are at church | 在教堂裏的婦女 |
| the children next to her | 她旁邊的孩子 |
| the children who are next to her | 在她旁邊的孩子 |
| the teachers in that room | 那室內的教師 |
| the teachers who are in that room | 在那室內的教師 |
| the students in the school | 學校裏的學生 |
| the students who are in the school | 在學校裏的學生 |

# Exercise 8

把下列句子轉為正確的時態：

1. He (go) to church on Sundays.

_____

2. It (rain) now.

_____

3. I (meet) him on the street yesterday.

_____

4. I (never be) to New York before.

_____

5. He (leave) Hong Kong next month.

_____

6. He (listen) to the radio when I come into the room.

_____

7. John and Mary always (go) to the cinema together.

_____

8. He (live) in Hong Kong since he was born.

_____

9. Tom (not arrive) yet.

_____

10. She (sing) beautifully in the concert last night.

_____

# THE INTERNATIONAL PHONETIC ALPHABET

## 國際音標

### 本課目標

國際音標（簡稱 IPA）是用來標示發音（指單音或音素）的語音符號系統，適用於所有語言中的語音。大部分英文辭典字典和教科書都是用這套符號。

# 母音

母音是音素的一種，與子音相對，也叫做元音。是在發音過程中由氣流通過口腔而不受阻礙發出的音。發音時，氣流從肺部通過喉部，使聲帶發出均勻震動，然後震音氣流不受阻礙的通過口腔、鼻腔，通過舌、唇的調節而發出不同的聲音。

🎧 1701.mp3

| | | | | |
|---|---|---|---|---|
| /iː/ | tea /tiː/ | 茶 | sleep /sliːp/ | 睡覺 |
| /ɪ/ | sit /sɪt/ | 坐下 | this /ðɪt/ | 這個 |
| /e/ | set /set/ | 落下 | desk /desk/ | 書桌 |
| /æ/ | bad /æ/ | 壞的 | fact /fækt/ | 事實 |
| /ɑː/ | art /ɑːt/ | 藝術 | arm /ɑːm/ | 手臂 |
| /ɒ/ | hot /hɒt/ | 熱的 | box /bɒks/ | 盒子 |
| /ɔː/ | draw /drɔː/ | 拉、牽 | caught /kɔːt/ | 捉住 |
| /ʊ/ | book /bʊk/ | 書 | put /pʊt/ | 置放 |
| /uː/ | moon /muːn/ | 月亮 | food /fuːd/ | 食物 |
| /ʌ/ | tub /tʌb/ | 桶 | cut /kʌt/ | 割開 |
| /ɜː/ | bird /bɜːd/ | 鳥 | first /fɜːst/ | 第一 |
| /ə/ | doctor /ˈdɒktə/ | 醫生 | ago /əˈgəʊ/ | 以前 |
| /eɪ/ | day /deɪ/ | 日間 | take /teɪk/ | 帶去 |
| /əʊ/ | go /gəʊ/ | 去 | coat /kəʊt/ | 外套 |
| /aɪ/ | light /laɪt/ | 光線 | time /taɪm/ | 時間 |
| /aʊ/ | now /naʊ/ | 現在 | mouth /maʊθ/ | 嘴巴 |
| /ɔɪ/ | boy /bɔɪ/ | 男孩子 | boil /bɔil/ | 沸騰 |
| /ɪə/ | hear /hɪə/ 見 | 聽 | beer /bɪə/ | 啤酒 |
| /ɛə/ | there /ðɛə/ | 那兒 | chair /ʃɛə/ | 椅子 |
| /ʊə/ | poor /pʊə/ | 貧窮 | tour /tʊə/ | 旅行 |

## /iː/

/i/ 發音時嘴唇微開成扁形，牙床近於閉合狀態，舌尖抵下齒，嘴邊肌肉向兩邊用力，音較長。例字：see /si /，feel /fiːl/。

## /ɪ/

/ ɪ / 發音時唇形扁平而自然，牙床近於半合，舌尖抵下齒，唇邊肌肉不用力，音短。例字：it /ɪt/，bit /bɪt/。

## /e/

/e/ 發音時嘴比在發 /ɪ/ 音時略為張開，嘴唇肌肉略向兩邊用力，舌尖不抵住牙齒，音短。例字：red /red/，dead /ded/。

## /æ/

/æ/ 發音時嘴比在發 /e/ 音時更張開，牙床處於開與半開之間，舌尖抵下齒。例字：man /mæn/，fat /fæt/。

## /ɑː/

/ɑː/ 音是英語母音中嘴張得最開的一個音，舌收平而用力，牙床全開，舌尖一般不抵下齒，音長而響亮。例字：art /ɑːt/，dark /dɑːk/。

## /ɒ/

/ɒ/ 發音時雙唇略圓，牙床全開，舌向後收，而且舌的位置很低，舌尖離開下齒，音短。例字：pot /pɒt/，rock /rɒk/。

## /ɔː/

/ɔː/ 發音時口形比發 /ɒ/ 音時更圓，雙唇稍突出，舌向後縮，音較長。例字：all /ɔːl/，law /lɔː/。

國際音標

135

## /ʊ/

/ʊ/ 發音時兩唇成圓形突出，發音時不用力，舌後的前部抬起，舌尖離開下齒，音短。例字：full /fʊl/，good /gʊd/。

## /uː/

/uː/ 發音時嘴唇尖而圓，雙唇向前突出，近於全閉的狀態，整個舌頭在口腔後部，舌尖離開下齒，並用力向後收，音長。例字：noon /nuːn/，roof /ruːf/。

## /ʌ/

/ʌ/ 發音時咀半開，雙唇向兩邊略張，舌尖抵下牙齦，音短。例字：but /bʌt/，luck /lʌk/。

## /ɜː/

/ɜː/ 發音時雙唇突出，嘴形圓，舌中面隆起，舌尖抵下齦，音長。例字：her /hɜː/，turn /tɜːn/。

## /ə/

/ə/ 是母音音素中發音最短的一個。發音時嘴半開，舌頭在自然的位置，音響低而弱。例字：sister /ˈsɪstə/，summer /ˈsʌmə/。

## /eɪ/

/eɪ/ 的發音由 /e/ 音向 /ɪ/ 音滑動，但未到 /ɪ/ 音的位置便停止了。例字：way /weɪ/，late /leɪt/。

## /əʊ/

/əʊ/ 的發音由 /o/ 音向 /ʊ/ 音滑動，唇形開始時半開而略圓，結束時則為閉圓。例字：home /həʊm/，low /ləʊ/。

## /aɪ/

/aɪ/ 音裏面的 /a/ 音不能單獨使用。發 /a/ 與 /ɑ:/ 音不同的地方，是以舌尖抵下齒。發/aɪ/音時由/a/向/ɪ/滑動。例字：five /faɪv/，pie /paɪ/。

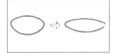

## /aʊ/

/aʊ/ 的發音由 /a/ 音向 /ʊ/ 音滑動。例字：house /haʊs/，cow /kaʊ/。

## /ɔɪ/

/ɔɪ/ 的發音由 /ɔ/ 音向 /ɪ/ 音滑動。例字：oil /ɔɪl/，toy /tɔɪ/。

## /ɪə/

/ɪə/ 的發音由 /ɪ/ 音向 /ə/ 音滑動。例字：cheer /tsɪə/，here /hɪə/。

## /ɛə/

/ɛə/ 裏面的 /ɛ/ 音很少單獨用，是介乎 /e/ 和 /æ/ 之間的音，只要發 /e/ 音時，口稍張開，舌稍向後收，便可發出/ɛ/音，再向/ə/滑動，即發出/ɛə/音。例字：pair /pɛə/，hair /hɛə/。

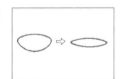

## /ʊə/

/ʊə/ 的發音由 /ʊ/ 音向 /ə/ 音滑動。例字：sure /ʃʊə/，pure /pjʊə/。

國際音標

# 子音

子音也是音素的一類，與母音相對，也叫做輔音。發音時氣流在發音器官某一部分受到阻礙。發子音時，氣流從肺中呼出，經過口腔、鼻腔時，受到唇、牙齒、舌頭、咽喉等阻礙而發出的不同聲音。

🎧 1702.mp3

| /p/ | pen /pen/ | 鉛筆 | stop /stɒp/ | 停 |
| /b/ | back /bæk/ | 在後面 | rob /rɒb/ | 搶奪 |
| /t/ | ten /ten/ | 十 | boot /bu:t/ | 長靴 |
| /d/ | doll /dɒl/ | 洋娃娃 | hand /hænd/ | 手 |
| /k/ | cock /kɒk/ | 公雞 | key /ki:/ | 鑰匙 |
| /g/ | dog /dɒg/ | 狗 | girl /gɜ:l/ | 女孩子 |
| /m/ | man /mæn/ | 男人 | comb /kəʊm/ | 梳子 |
| /n/ | name /neɪm/ | 名字 | nine /naɪn/ | 九 |
| /n/ | king /kɪŋ/ | 皇帝 | English /'ɪŋglɪʃ/ | 英文 |
| /l/ | long /lɒŋ/ | 長的 | still /stɪl/ | 仍然 |
| /f/ | feel /fi:l/ | 感覺 | knife /naɪf/ | 刀 |
| /v/ | vase /ve:z/ | 花瓶 | live /lɪv/ | 生存 |
| /θ/ | thin /θin/ | 瘦的，薄的 | warmth /wɔ:mθ/ | 溫暖 |

| /ð/ | these /ði:z/ | 這些 | mother /'mʌðə/ | 母親 |
| /s/ | sun /sʌn/ | 太陽 | face /feɪs/ | 臉 |
| /z/ | zero /'zɪərəʊ/ | 零 | nose /nəʊz/ | 鼻子 |
| /ʃ/ | she /ʃi:/ | 她 | wish /wɪʃ/ | 願望 |
| /ʒ/ | rouge /ru:ʒ/ | 胭脂 | pleasure /'pleʒə/ | 快樂 |
| /r/ | roof /ru:f/ | 屋頂 | very/'verɪ/ | 十分 |
| /h/ | head /hed/ | 頭 | high /haɪ/ | 高 |
| /ʧ/ | chalk /ʧɔ:k/ | 粉筆 | reach /ri:ʧ/ | 到達 |
| /ʤ/ | jump /ʤʌmp/ | 跳 | jam /ʤæm/ | 果醬 |
| /w/ | we /wi:/ | 我們 | wet /wet/ | 潮濕 |
| /j/ | yes /jes/ | 是的 | young /jʌŋ/ | 年輕的 |

國際音標

# 英語子音發音圖解

## /p/、/b/

/p/屬雙唇音。發音時先將兩唇輕閉，然後略為用力把口腔中的氣噴出，出聲時不振動聲帶。例字：peak /piːk/，step /step/。

/b/的發音方法大致與/p/相同，但噴氣時聲帶振動。例字：back /bæk/，bribe /braɪb/。

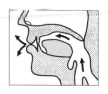

## /t/、/d/

/t/發音時嘴微張，舌尖抵在上牙齦，然後稍微用力把舌尖彈開，使氣流衝出而發出的破裂音，發音時聲帶不振動，例字：tax /tæks/，late /leɪt/。

/d/的發音方法大致與/t/相同，但發音時聲帶振動。例字：date /deɪt/，hide /haɪd/。

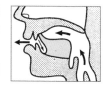

## /k/、/g/

/k/發音時嘴微開，舌後部抬高，使氣流不能入口腔內，然後用力將舌部彈開，使氣流急速衝出而發出破裂音，聲帶不振動。例字：cake /keɪk/，kite /kaɪt/。

/g/發音方法大致與/k/相同，但發音時聲帶振動。例字：girl /gɜːl/，pig /pɪg/。

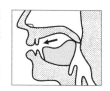

## /m/

/m/發音時雙唇緊閉，舌在自然的位置，振動聲帶，並使氣流通入鼻腔，然後從鼻孔逸出。例字：mark /mɑːk/，him /hɪm/。

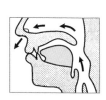

## /n/

/n/發音時嘴微開，舌尖抵上牙齦以堵塞氣流，使氣流從鼻腔走出來，聲帶振動。例字：neck /nek/，pen /pen/。

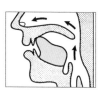

## /ŋ/

/ŋ/ 發音時口比發 /n/ 音較張開，舌抵上顎以堵住氣流進入口腔，通過鼻腔發出聲音，聲帶振動。例字：bring /briŋ/，think /θink/。

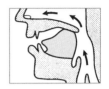

## /l/

/l/ 發音時嘴微張，舌尖抵上顎，然後把舌彈下，氣流從舌兩側逸出，聲帶振動。例字：let /let/，plan /plæn/。

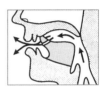

## /f/、/v/

/f/ 發音時上牙咬下唇，將氣流從口腔中吹出來，發音時聲帶不振動。例字：fail /feɪl/，staff /stɑːf/。

/v/ 發音方法與 /f/ 同，但發音時聲帶振動。例字：view /vjuː/，live /lɪv/。

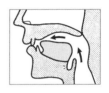

## /θ/、/ð/

/θ/ 發音時嘴微張，把舌尖伸出，放在上下牙縫之間，然後用力把舌頭縮入，使氣流由口腔中壓送出來。聲帶不振動。例字：thunder /'θʌndə/，throw /θrəʊ/。

/ð/ 發音方法與 /θ/ 相同，但發音時聲帶振動。例字：they /ðei/，gather /'gæðə/。

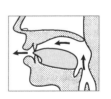

## /s/、/z/

/s/ 發音時上下牙合攏但不相碰，雙唇微開，舌尖抵上牙齦，然後將氣流從口腔內用力送出，聲帶不振動。例字：seat /siːt/，maps /mæps/。

/z/ 發音方法與 /s/ 相同，但發音時聲帶振動。例字：zoo /zuː/，noise /nɔɪz/。

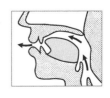

國際音標

## /ʃ/ 、 /ʒ/

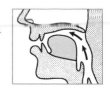

/ʃ/ 發音時雙唇突出作圓形，舌尖略為抬高，但不觸及上顎，然後用力將氣流自舌面和上下牙的空隙間吐出而發摩擦音。聲帶不振動。例字：sheep /siːp/，marsh /mɑːs/。

/ʒ/ 發音方法與 /s/ 相同，但發音時聲帶振動。例字：vision /'vɪʃən/，measure /'meʒə/。

## /r/

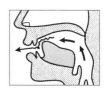

/r/ 發音時嘴微開，捲動舌頭而發出摩擦音，聲帶振動。例字：run /rʌn/，real /rɪəl/。

## /h/

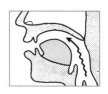

/h/ 發音時嘴半開，把氣流從氣管通過口腔噴出，聲帶不振動。例字：hill /hɪl/，hand /hænd/。

## /tʃ/ 、 /dʒ/

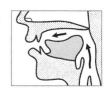

/tʃ/ 發音時雙唇向前突出，舌尖接近上牙齦，氣流從口腔內經舌面及雙唇間的空隙摩擦而成音。例字：cheap /tʃiːp/，march /mɑːtʃ/。

/dʒ/ 發音方法與 /tʃ/ 相同，但發音時聲帶振動。例字：joke /dʒəʊk/，judge /dʒʌdʒ/。

## /w/ 、 /j/

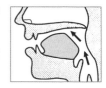

/w/ 發音時雙唇突出作圓形，然後向兩邊拉開，聲帶振動。例字：weak /wiːk/，which /wɪtʃ/。

/j/ 發音時嘴微張，口形和發 /iː/ 音時相似。然後嘴向下拉，讓氣流從舌面吹出，聲帶振動。例字：year /jɪə/，few /fjuː/。

# 練習答案

❶ It's a pen.
❷ It's an egg.
❸ It's a table.
❹ It's a chair.
❺ It's an apple.

❶ Yes, it is.
❷ No, it isn't.
❸ No, it isn't.
❹ Yes, it is.
❺ No, it isn't.

❶ You're a doctor.
❷ She's a nurse.
❸ He's a clerk.
❹ They're students.
❺ We're boys.

❶ Are you a boy?
❷ Is she a girl?
❸ Are you doctors?
❹ Are you Tom?
❺ Are they teachers?

❶ Yes, I am.
❷ No, I'm not.
❸ No, he isn't.
❹ Yes, you are.
❺ Yes, they are.

❶ It's my book.
❷ It's his pencil.
❸ It's her coat.
❹ It's our car.
❺ It's their house.

❶ It's theirs.
❷ It's his.
❸ It's ours.
❹ It's yours.
❺ It's hers.

1. He goes to church on Sundays.
2. It Is raining now.
3. I met him on the street yesterday.
4. I've never been to New York before.
5. He will leave Hong Kong next month.
6. He is listening to the radio when I come into the room.
7. John and Mary always go to the cinema together.
8. He has lived in Hong Kong since he was born.
9. Tom hasn't arrived yet.
10. She sang beautifully in the concert last night.